BLEEDERS

"Nameless Detective" Mysteries by
BILL PRONZINI

BLEEDERS

A
"Nameless Detective"
Novel

Bill Pronzini

CARROLL & GRAF PUBLISHERS
NEW YORK

BLEEDERS

Carroll & Graf Publishers
An Imprint of Avalon Publishing Group Inc.
161 William St., 16th Floor
New York, NY 10038

First Carroll & Graf edition 2002

Library of Congress Cataloging-in-Publication Data is
available.

ISBN: 0-7867-0942-1

Printed in the United States of America
Distributed by Publishers Group West

For Bill Pronzini
Without whom this series would
never have been written

BLEEDERS

1

I LAID A RED QUEEN ON A BLACK KING, glanced up at Jay Cohalan through the door to his private cubicle. He was pacing again, side wall to side window across the front of his desk, his hands in constant restless motion at his sides. The cubicle was carpeted; his footfalls made no sound. There was no discernible sound anywhere except for the faint snap and slap when I turned over a card and put it down. An office building at night is one of the quietest places there is. Eerily so, if you spend enough time listening to the silence.

Trey. Nine of diamonds. Deuce. Jack of spades. I was marrying the jack to a red queen when Cohalan quit pacing and came over to stand in the doorway. He watched me for a time, his hands still doing scoop-shovel maneuvers. Big man in his late thirties, handsome except for a weak chin, his dusty brown hair and tan suit disheveled. A sheen of sweat coated his cheeks and upper lip, even though it was not warm in there.

"How can you just sit there playing cards?" he said.

There were several answers to that. Years of stakeouts and dull routine had taught me a certain grudging patience. We'd only been waiting about an hour. The money, seventy-five thousand dollars in hundred-dollar bills, didn't belong to me. I was neither worried nor upset, nor afraid that something might go wrong. But I passed on all of that and settled instead for a neutral response.

"Solitaire's good for waiting," I said. "Keeps your mind off the clock."

"It's after seven. Why the hell doesn't he call?"

"You know the answer to that."

"Yeah. He wants me to sweat."

"And you're obliging him."

"For Christ's sake, I can't help it. I'm scared, man."

"I know it."

"Sadistic bastard."

He didn't mean me, so I said, "Blackmail's that kind of game. Torture the victim, bend his will to yours."

"Game. My God." Cohalan came out into the anteroom and began to pace around there, in front of his secretary's desk where I was sitting. "It's driving me crazy, trying to figure out who he is, how he found out about my past."

"Any luck?"

"No. He didn't give me a hint, any of the times I talked to him. But he knows everything, every damn detail."

"You'll have the answers before long."

Cohalan stopped abruptly, leaned toward me. "Listen, this has to be the end of it. You've got to stay with him tonight, make sure he's arrested. I can't take any more."

"I'll do my job, don't worry."

"Seventy-five thousand dollars," he said. "I almost had a heart attack when he told me that was how much he wanted this time. The last payment . . . balloon payment, he called it. What a crock. He'll come back for more some day. I know it, Carolyn knows it, you know it." Pacing again. "Poor Carolyn. She's so high-strung, emotional . . . it's been even harder on her."

I turned a card. Spade nine. I laid it on a ten of diamonds and squared the edges.

Cohalan said, "She wanted me to go the police in the beginning, did I tell you that? Practically begged me."

"You told me."

"I should have, I guess. Now I've got to pay a middleman for what I could've had done for nothing. No offense."

"None taken."

"I just couldn't bring myself to do it, walk into the Hall of Justice and confess my sins to a cop. It was hard enough letting Carolyn talk me into hiring a private detective."

Black four. No help.

"That trouble when I was a kid . . . it's a criminal offense; I could still be prosecuted for it. And it's liable to cost me my job if it comes out. I went through hell telling Carolyn when the blackmail started, couldn't force myself to go into the more sordid details. Not with you, either. The police . . . no, never. I know that bastard will probably spill the whole story when he's in custody, try to drag me down with him, but I keep hoping it won't happen. A miracle's all I've got left to cling to, like a drowning man clinging to a stick. You know what I mean?"

"I know what you mean," I said.

"I shouldn't't've paid him when he crawled out of the woodwork eight months ago. I know that now. But back then it seemed like the only way to keep my life from being ruined. Carolyn thought so, too. If I hadn't started paying him, half of her inheritance wouldn't already be gone."

Ace of clubs. I put that card down, added the deuce off the pile. I wasn't winning, just holding my own—about all you can expect in most games of solitaire. And what most of us learn to settle for in living our lives.

Cohalan paced in silence for a time, stopped to stare out through the window at the fog-misted lights of the city, then started up again—pacing and talking both. "I hated taking money from her.

3

Hated it, no matter how much she kept insisting it belongs to both of us. And I hate myself for doing it, almost as much as I hate him. All my fault, start to finish. But goddamn it, blackmail's the worst crime there is, short of murder."

"Not the worst," I said, "but bad enough."

"This *has* to be the end of it. That seventy-five thousand in there . . . it's the last of her money, our money. All our savings sitting right there in that briefcase. If that son of a bitch gets away with it, we'll be wiped out. You can't let that happen."

I didn't say anything. We'd been through all this before, too many times.

He said, "I've got to take a leak—my bladder feels like it's ready to pop. John's just down the hall, I won't be two minutes. If the phone rings . . ."

"I'll handle it, don't worry."

"Two minutes," he said and went out at a half run.

He was gone three. I was dealing myself a new hand when he came back. "Not yet," I said.

"Shit."

He stood over me, breathing heavily through his nose. Abruptly he said, "This job of mine, you'd think it pays pretty well, wouldn't you? My own office, secretary, executive title, expense account . . . looks good and sounds good, but it's a frigging dead end. Junior account executive stuck in corporate middle management—that's all I am or ever will be. There're already rumors the company's going to downsize. If that happens, I'll be one of the first to go."

"No other prospects?"

"Not any that'll pay what I'm making now. Sixty thousand gross. And Carolyn makes twenty-five teaching those music courses of hers. Eighty-five thousand for two people, no kids, that seems like plenty, but it's not—not these days and sure as hell not in San Francisco. Dot-com paradise, that's what the city's become, cost of living's through the roof. Add taxes, mortgage payments, all the rest of it, you have to scrimp like hell to put anything away. And then some stupid mistake you made when you were a kid comes back to haunt you, starts draining what little you've got to keep you solvent . . . you understand, right? But I didn't see where I had a choice at first. I was afraid of going to prison, afraid of losing this dead-end job before they throw me out. Caught between a rock and a hard place. I still feel that way, but now I don't care, I just want that scumbag to get what's coming to him. . . ."

Repetitious babbling. His mouth had a wet look, and his gaze kept jumping from me to other points in the anteroom. His irises were as bright as blue-veined marbles.

I said, "Why don't you sit down?"

"I can't sit. My nerves are shot."

"You're making me nervous."

"I can't sit, I tell you. Why doesn't he call? It's already seven . . . seven o'clock. . . ."

"Take a few shallow breaths before you start to hyperventilate."

"Listen, don't tell me what—"

The telephone on his desk went off.

The sudden clamor jerked him half around, as if with an electric shock. In the quiet that followed, the first thing I could hear was the irregular rasp of his breathing. He looked back at me as the bell sounded again. I was on my feet, too, by then.

"Go ahead, answer it," I told him. "Keep your head."

He went into his office, picked up just after the third ring. I timed the lifting of the secretary's phone to coincide, so there would not be a second click on the open line.

"Yes," he said, "Cohalan."

"You know who this is." The voice was harsh, muffled, indistinctively male. "You got the money?"

"I told you I'd have it. This is the last, you promised me. . . ."

"Seventy-five thousand, and you never hear from me again."

"Where this time?"

"Golden Gate Park. Kennedy Drive, by the buffalo pen. Put it in the trash barrel beside the bench there."

Cohalan was watching me through the open doorway. I shook my head at him. He said into the phone, "Can't we make it someplace else? What if there're people around?"

"Just do what you're told. Nine P.M. sharp."

"Nine? That's two hours . . ."

"Be there. With the cash."

The line went dead.

I cradled the secretary's phone. Cohalan was still standing alongside his desk, hanging onto his receiver, when I moved into the cubicle.

"Put it down, Mr. Cohalan."

"What? Oh . . . yes." The receiver slid from his fingers, made a clattering noise in the cradle. "Christ," he said then.

"You all right?"

His head bobbed up and down a couple of times. He ran a hand over his face, yanked hard on his lower lip, and then swung away to where the big cowhide briefcase lay. The cash was packed in there; he'd shown it to me when I first arrived. He picked up the case, set it down again. Rubbed and yanked at his face another time.

"Maybe I shouldn't risk the money," he said.

He wasn't talking to me so I made no answer.

"I could leave it right here where it'll be safe. Stick a phone book or something in the case for weight." He sank into his chair; popped up again like a jack-in-the-box. "No, what's the matter with me; that won't work. I'm not thinking straight. He might open the case in the park. No telling what he'd do if the money's not there. And he's got to have it when the police come. Right? In his possession?"

"Yes."

"All right. But for God's sake don't let him get away with it."

"He won't get away with it."

Another jerky nod. "When're you leaving?"

"Right now," I said. "You stay put until at least eight-thirty. It won't take you more than twenty minutes to get out to the park."

"I don't know if I can get through another hour of waiting around here."

"Keep telling yourself it'll be over soon. Get yourself calmed down. The state you're in now, you shouldn't be behind the wheel."

"I'll be okay."

"Come straight back here after you make the drop. You'll hear from me as soon as I have anything to report."

"Just don't make me wait too long," Cohalan said. And then, again and to himself, "I'll be okay."

Cohalan's office building was on Kearney, not far from where Kerry works at the Bates and Carpenter ad agency on lower Geary. She was on my mind, as she often is, as I drove down to Geary and turned west toward the park. Emily, too—sweet, troubled little Emily. My thoughts prompted me to lift the car phone and call the condo. The sitter answered; Kerry wasn't home yet. Like me, she puts in a lot of overtime night work. A wonder we manage to spend as much time together as we do . . . as much time with Emily as we do, jointly and separately. Which was part of the problem, of course. A bigger part than we'd anticipated and one that was not easily solved.

I tried her private number at B and C and got her voice mail. In transit, probably, the same as I was: Two among the many sets of headlights crossing the dark city just now. Urban night riders, that was us. Except that she was going home, and I was on my way to nail a shakedown artist for a paying client.

That started me thinking about the kind of work I do. One of the downsides of urban night riding is that it gives vent to introspection and, sometimes, dark self-analysis. Skip traces, insurance claims investigations, employee background checks—they're the meat of my business. There used to be some challenge to jobs like that, some creative maneuvering required, but nowadays it's little more than routine legwork (mine) and a lot of computer time (Tamara Corbin, my techno-whiz assistant). I don't get to use my head as much as I once did. My problem, in Tamara's Generation X opinion, was that I was a "retro private eye," pining away for the old days and old ways. True enough; I never have adapted well to change. The detective racket just isn't as stimulating or satisfying after thirty-plus years and with a new set of rules.

Every now and then, though, a case comes along that stirs the juices—one with some spark and sizzle and a much higher satisfaction level than the run-of-the-mill stuff. I live for cases like that; they're what keep me from packing it in, taking an early retirement at age sixty. They usually involve a felony of some sort and sometimes a whisper if not a shout of danger, and they allow me to use my full complement of functioning brain cells. This Cohalan case, for instance. This one I liked, because bleeders—the blackmailers and extortionists and small-time grifters and other sociopathic opportunists who prey on the weak and gullible—are near the top of my list of worthless parasites, and I enjoy hell out of taking one down.

Yeah, *this* case I liked a whole lot.

2

GOLDEN GATE PARK HAS PLENTY OF daytime attractions—museums, tiny lakes, rolling lawns and playing fields, windmills, an arboretum—but on a foggy November night it's a mostly empty place to pass through on your way to somewhere else.

It does have its night denizens, of course, like any large park in any large city: homeless squatters, not all of whom are harmless, and predators on the prowl through its sprawling acres of shadows and nightshapes. On a night like this it also has an atmosphere of lonely isolation, the shifting fog hiding city lights and turning streetlamps and passing headlights into surreal blurs.

The buffalo enclosure is at the westward end, less than a mile from the ocean—the least-traveled section of the park after about eight P.M. There were no cars in the vicinity, moving or parked, when I came down Kennedy Drive. My lights picked out the fence on the north side, the rolling pastureland beyond; the trash barrel and bench were about halfway along, at the edge of the bicycle path that parallels the road.

I drove past there, looking for a place to park and wait. I didn't want to sit on Kennedy Drive; a lone car close to the drop point would be too conspicuous. I had to do this right. If anything did not seem kosher, the whole thing might fail to go down the way it was supposed to.

The ideal spot came up fifty yards or so from the trash barrel, opposite the buffaloes' feeding corral—a narrow road that led to Anglers Lodge where the city maintains casting pools for fly fishermen to practice on. Nobody was likely to go up there at night, and trees and shrubbery bordered one side, the shadows in close to them thickly clotted. Kennedy Drive was still empty in both directions, so I cut in past the Anglers Lodge sign and drove up the road until I found a place where I could turn around. Then I shut off my lights, made the U-turn, and coasted back down into the heavy shadows. From there I could see the drop point clearly enough, even with the low-riding fog. I shut off the engine, slumped down on the seat with my back against the door.

No detective, public or private, likes stakeouts. Dull, boring, dead time that can be a literal pain in the ass if it goes on long enough. This one wasn't too bad because it would be short, only about an hour, but time lagged and crawled just the same. I kept my eyes off my watch, not that that did any good. I'd been doing this kind of thing for so many years I could almost hear the retarded ticking-off of the seconds inside my head. One . . . two . . . three. . . .

Kerry and Emily were still foremost in my mind. Another call to the condo? Kerry might be home by now. If not, I could talk to the kid; it wasn't her bedtime yet. That was where she'd be, though, in her room with Shameless the cat, listening to music or reading or fooling around with her computer or maybe just staring off into space. She spent more and more time in there, drawn deep inside herself. Communication had become increasingly difficult. It wasn't that she was despondent or dissatisfied with us, her new school, her new life. She was simply not there much of the time. Lost or maybe hiding in a place neither Kerry nor I nor anyone else could go.

So what would I say to her if I called now? "Hi, I'm sitting out here in the fog in Golden Gate Park, getting ready to catch some bad guys, and I just thought I'd call and see if you're all right and remind you to brush your teeth before you go to sleep." She didn't need to hear my disembodied voice on the phone. She needed me there with her, to hold her and try again, lamely if earnestly, to make her understand that her life wouldn't always be full of pain and loss and loneliness and uncertainty. To convince her that someday she'd be happy again.

Six months an orphan. Six months . . . not much time at all. Unless you're ten years old and everything you've known and believed in and trusted for those ten years has been ripped apart; the past and its relative comforts suddenly dead, the future impossible to imagine, and all you have to cling to in the present is a couple of relative strangers old enough to be your grandparents but with no experience whatsoever in raising a child your age or in finding meaningful ways to give you the constant reassurance you need. In that case, it was a hell of a long time. It might even seem like a piece of forever.

Hard. So damn hard for all of us. Cybil, Kerry's mother, helped as much as she could, but Cybil was eighty years old and led an active and productive life of her own over in Marin County. Friends and neighbors had been helpful, too, dependable and supportive, but they were strangers seldom seen and even harder for a child to relate to. What Emily needed were full-time parents, and what she was getting was a collection of part-time caregivers. It wasn't nearly enough. And because it wasn't, the strain was starting to tell on everyone concerned.

The best thing would've been for either Kerry or me to quit working and devote the necessary time to Emily's welfare. But that was not going to happen. We'd been at our jobs too many years; we were too set in our ways; neither of us was that selfless. It had nothing to do with finances; money was not a motivating factor in our lives. We loved Emily, but we loved our work more because it defined us, sustained us, gave us purpose. At our ages we were simply incapable of making that kind of sacrifice. If one of us did, it would likely lead to resentment and do the child more harm than good.

But that didn't change the fact that we were committed to Emily, to the bargain we'd made. The right time for her to be handed over to Child Welfare, made a ward of the court, and put in a foster home had come and gone; we'd all of us seen to that. Emily by making it plain to all concerned, including the judge at the adoption hearing, that she did not want to live with anyone but Kerry and me. Cybil by working on us repeatedly, breaking down our reservations. The two of us by talking it out endlessly, waffling back and forth but knowing in our hearts we were soft touches and in the end would give in because it was what we wanted, too. Once we were granted custody, it was too late for any other viable alternative. To back out now, simply because we were having the problems we'd expected to have and had yet to find ways to bridge the wall of years and need, was unthinkable. We'd hate ourselves if we did that; and more importantly, abandoning Emily at this point might damage her almost as much as losing her real parents had. She was so fragile she might never recover.

So that was not going to happen, either. What would happen: We'd continue to do the best we could, take care of her and be there for her as often as we could, give her as much love and support as we knew how. The crisis period would ease eventually, the wounds would begin to heal as she grew toward adulthood. We had to believe that. No, not just believe it. Somehow we had to make it happen.

Sitting there in the dark, thinking these thoughts, added to my discomfort. Tick. Tock. Tick. Tock. Now and then a car drifted by, its headlights reflecting off rather than boring through the wall of mist. The ones heading west may have been able to see my car briefly in dark silhouette as they passed, but none happened to be a police patrol, and nobody else was curious enough or venal enough to stop and hassle me.

I shifted position for the tenth or twentieth time, to ease an incip-ient cramp in my right ham. A thin coating of fog-damp had formed on the windshield, so I turned on the ignition long enough to use the wipers. There was condensation on the inside of the glass, too, even though I had the driver's window rolled partway down; I cleared that away with my hand. Must be close to nine now, I thought. I gave in to the urge to check my watch. Right: six minutes to nine.

And that was when Cohalan showed up, predictably early because he was anxious to get this part of it over and done with.

He came barreling along Kennedy Drive too fast for the condi-tions; I heard the squeal of brakes as he swung over and rocked his white Camry to a stop near the trash receptacle. I watched the dark shape of him step out and run across the path, the heavy briefcase a squarish bulk banging against his leg. He made the drop, ran back at the same speed. Ten seconds later the Camry hissed past where I was hidden, again traveling too fast, and was gone.

Nine o'clock.

I sat upright now, a little tensed, both hands on the wheel.

Nine-o-five.

Headlights put a glare on the wet road surface, but they were high and bright—truck lights. An old stakebed rumbled past without slowing.

Nine-o-eight.

Another set of beams appeared, this one belonging to a small car heading east. As it approached, I saw that it was low-slung, dark-colored. Vintage MG. It rolled along slowly until it was opposite the barrel, then veered at a sudden sharp angle across the road, its brake lights flashing blood-red, and rocked to a stop. I reached out to tighten fingers around the ignition key. The door over there opened without a light coming on inside, and the driver jumped out in a hurry, indistinct in a coat and some kind of head covering; ran to the barrel, scooped out the briefcase, ran back, and hurled it inside.

I had the engine started and in gear as the driver hopped in. Fast takeoff, even faster than Cohalan had fled the scene, the sports car's rear end fishtailing slightly as the tires fought for traction on the slick pavement. I was out on Kennedy and in pursuit within seconds.

There was no way I could drive in the fog-laden darkness without putting on my lights. In the far reach of the beams I could see the other car a hundred yards or so ahead. But even when I accelerated, I couldn't get close enough to check the license plate.

Where the Drive forks on the east end of the buffalo enclosure, the MG made a tight-angle left turn, brake lights flaring again, headlight beams yawing as the driver fought for control. Scared, maybe stoned, and a little crazy to be driving so recklessly on this kind of night. I took the turn at about half the speed. I still had the MG in sight as we looped around Spreckels Lake toward the park exit on 36th Avenue, but it would have taken stunt-driver skills to catch up.

The stoplight at 36th and Fulton glowed a misty red when the sports job reached the exit. The driver, without slowing, made a sliding right turn through the red, narrowly missing one oncoming car and causing another to brake and skid sideways. The MG came close to spinning out of control and into a roll that probably would have killed the reckless damn fool at the wheel. Caught just enough traction as horns brayed angrily, and disappeared, swaying and roaring on Fulton to the east.

The near-accident shook me up a little. If I tried to continue pursuit, somebody—an innocent party, maybe—was liable to get hurt or killed, and that was the last thing I wanted to happen. High-speed car chases are for lunatics and the makers of trite action films. I pulled over to the side of the road, still inside the park, and sat there for a minute or so until my pulse rate slowed to normal. Thinking I should have anticipated something like this, should have handled the whole thing differently. Too late now. Be thankful that somebody *hadn't* got hurt or killed and that my overloaded conscience had been spared yet another heavy burden.

Cohalan threw a fit when I rang him on the car phone and told him what had happened. He called me all kinds of names, the least offensive of which was "incompetent idiot." I let him rant. There were no excuses to be made and no point in wasting my own breath.

He ran out of abuse finally and segued into his old self-pitying lament. "What am I going to do now? What am I going to tell Carolyn? All our savings gone, and I still don't have any idea who that blackmailing bastard is. What if he comes back for more? We couldn't even sell the house, there's hardly any equity. . . ."

Pretty soon he ran down again. I waited through about five seconds of dead air. Then he said, "All right," followed the words with a gusty sigh, and added, "But don't expect me to pay your bill. You can damn well sue me, and you can't get blood out of a turnip." He banged the receiver in my ear.

Some Cohalan. Some piece of work.

And now, by God, it was *my* turn.

3

THE APARTMENT BUILDING WAS ON LOCUST Street a half block off California and close to the Presidio. Built in the twenties, judging from its ornate brick-and-plaster facade; once somebody's modestly affluent private home, long ago cut up into three floors of studios and one-bedroom apartments. It had no garage, forcing its tenants—like most of those in the neighboring buildings—into street parking.

I drove by slowly, looking for two things: a parking place and the low-slung black MG. I found the car easily enough—it was squeezed into a too-narrow space at the end of the block, its front wheels canted up onto the sidewalk—but there wasn't space for my car on that block, or the next, or anywhere in the vicinity. Back on California, I quit hunting and pulled into a bus zone. If I got a ticket, I got a ticket.

Not much chance I'd need a weapon for the rest of it, but sometimes trouble comes when you least expect it. So I unclipped the .38 Colt Bodyguard from under the dash, slipped it into my coat pocket before I stepped out.

The building on Locust had a tiny foyer with the usual row of built-in mailboxes. I found the button for 2-C, leaned on it. This was the ticklish part; I was banking on the fact that one voice sounds pretty much like another over an intercom. Turned out not to be an issue: The squawk box stayed silent and the door release buzzed instead. Cocky. Hyped on drugs, adrenaline, or both. And just plain greedy-stupid.

I pushed inside, climbed the stairs to the second floor. Apartment 2-C was the first on the right. The door opened just as I reached it, and Annette Byers poked her head out and said with shiny-eyed excitement, "You made real good—"

The rest of it snapped off when she got a clear look at me; the excitement gave way to confusion and sudden alarm, froze her with the door half open. I had time to move up on her, wedge my shoulder against the door before she could decide to jump back and slam it in my face. She let out a bleat and tried to kick me as I crowded her inside. I caught her arms, then gave her a shove to get clear of her, and nudged the door closed with my heel.

"I'll start screaming," she said. Shaky bravado, the kind without anything to back it up. Fright showed through the bright glaze in her eyes. "These walls are paper thin, and I got a neighbor who's a cop."

That last was a lie. I said, "Go ahead. Be my guest."

"Who the hell do you think you are—"

"You know who I am, Annette. And why I'm here. The reason's on the table over there."

In spite of herself, she glanced to her left. The apartment was a none-too-clean or tidy studio, and the kitchenette and dining area were on that side. The big cowhide briefcase sat on the dinette table, its lid raised. I couldn't see inside from where I stood, but then I didn't need to.

"I don't know what you're talking about," she said.

She hadn't been back very long; she still wore the heavy coat and a wool stocking cap that completely hid her streaky blond hair. Her cheeks were flushed—the cold night, money, lust, methamphetamine, now fear. She was attractive enough in a too-ripe way, intelligent enough to hold down a job with a neighborhood travel service, and immoral enough to have been in trouble with the law before this. Twenty-three, single, and a crankhead: She'd been arrested once for possession and once for trying to peddle meth to an undercover cop. Crystal meth, the worst kind there is.

"Counting the cash, right?" I said.

" . . . What?"

"What you were doing when I rang the bell. It's all there—seven hundred and fifty hundred-dollar bills, according to plan."

"I don't know what you're talking about."

"You said that already."

"Fuck you."

"Uh-huh."

I moved a little to get a better scan of the studio. Sitting area on my left, sleeping arrangement behind that with a Chinese-style folding screen hiding the bed. I located the telephone on the breakfast bar that partitioned off the kitchenette, one of those cordless types with a built-in answering machine. The gadget beside it was a portable cassette recorder. She hadn't bothered to put the recorder away before leaving tonight; there'd been no reason to. The tape would still be inside.

I looked at her again. "I've got to admit, you handle that MG pretty well. Reckless as hell, though, the way you went flying out of the park on a red light."

"I don't know what you're talking about."

"You came damn close to causing a fatal accident. If you had, you'd be facing a manslaughter charge right now. Think about that."

"I don't know what—" She broke off and backed away a couple of paces, one hand rubbing the side of her face, her tongue making snakelike flicks between her lips. It was sinking in, how it had all gone wrong, how much trouble she was in. "You couldn't've followed me. I *know* you didn't."

"That's right, I couldn't and I didn't."

"Then how—?"

"Think about that, too. You'll figure it out."

Silence. And then sudden comprehension, like a low-wattage bulb coming on behind her eyes. "You . . . you knew about me all along."

"You, the plan, everything."

"The plan? But . . . how could you? I don't—"

The downstairs bell made a sudden racket. Her gaze jerked past me to the intercom unit next to the door. She sucked in her lower lip, bit down hard on it.

"Now I wonder who that can be," I said.

"Oh God . . ."

"Don't use the intercom, just the door release."

She did what I told her, moving as if her joints had begun to stiffen. I went the other way, first to the breakfast bar where I popped the tape out of the cassette player and slipped it into my pocket, then to the dinette table. I lowered the lid on the briefcase, fastened the catches. I had the case in my left hand when she turned to face me again.

She said, "What're you gonna do with the money?"

"Give it back to its rightful owner."

"Jay. It belongs to him."

"Like hell it does."

"Try to keep it for yourself, I'll bet that's what you're really gonna do."

I had nothing to say to that.

"Well, it won't happen." She stamped her foot. "You hear me? You don't have any right to that money!"

"You dumb-ass kid," I said disgustedly, "neither do you."

She quit looking at me. When she made to open the door I told her no, to wait for his knock. She stood with her back to me, shoulders hunched, face pale.

Knuckles on the door. She opened it then without hesitation, and he blew in talking fast the way he did when he was keyed up. "Oh, baby, baby, we did it, we pulled it off."

"Shit! You're not supposed to be here now. . . ."

"I know, but I couldn't wait." He grabbed her, started to pull her against him. And that was when he saw me.

"Hello, Cohalan," I said.

He went rigid for about five seconds, then disentangled himself from Byers and stood gawping at me. His mouth worked, but nothing came out. Manic as hell in his office, talking a blue streak—nerves and a hit or two of speed. He was a crankhead the same as her; that was the real reason he'd gone out to the john earlier. But facing me now, he was speechless. Lies were easy for him; the truth would have to be dragged out.

I told him to close the door. He did it automatically and then swung snarling on Annette Byers.

"You let him follow you here!"

"I didn't. He already knew about me. He knows everything."

"No, how could—"

"You stupid dickhead, you didn't fool him for a minute. Not for a minute."

"Shut up!" His eyes shifted to me. "Don't listen to her. She's the one who's been blackmailing me, she—"

"Knock it off, Cohalan," I said. "Nobody's been blackmailing you. You two are the bleeders—a cute little shakedown to steal your wife's money. You couldn't just grab the bundle without facing theft charges, and you couldn't get any of it by divorcing her because a spouse's inheritance isn't community property. So you cooked up the phony blackmail scam. What were you planning to do with the cash? Try to run it up into a big score in the stock market or in Vegas? Buy a load of crystal meth for resale, maybe?"

"You see?" Byers said bitterly. "He knows *everything.*"

Cohalan waggled his head. He'd gotten over his initial shock and he looked stricken; his hands had started that scoop-shovel trick at his sides. "You believed me. I know you did."

"Wrong," I said. "I didn't believe you. I'm a better actor than you, is all. Your story didn't sound right from the first. Too elaborate, loaded with improbabilities. Seventy-five thousand is much too large a blackmail bite for any past crime short of murder, and you swore to me—your wife, too—you weren't guilty of a major felony. Blackmailers seldom work in big bites anyway. They bleed their victims in small bites to keep them from throwing the hook. We just didn't buy it, either of us."

"We? Jesus, you mean . . . you and Carolyn. . . ."

"That's right. You were never my client, Cohalan—it's been your wife all along. Why do you think I never asked you for a retainer? Or suggested we mark the money just in case?"

He muttered something and pawed his face.

"She showed up at my office right after you did the first time," I said. "If she hadn't, I'd have gone to her myself. She's been suspicious all along, and when you hit her with the big bite, she figured it for a scam right away. She thought you might be having an affair, that that's where the money was going. Didn't take me long to find out about Annette. You never had a clue you were being followed, did you? Once I knew about her, it was easy enough to put the rest of it together, including the business with the money drop tonight." I showed him my teeth. "And here we are."

"Damn you," he said, but there was no heat in the words. "You and that frigid bitch both."

He wasn't referring to Annette Byers, but she took the opportunity to dig into him again. "Wise guy. I *told* you it was a bad idea to hire a goddamn private cop—"

"Shut up, for God's sake."

"Don't keep telling me to shut up."

"Shut up shut up shut up!"

"You son of a—"

"Don't say it. I'll slap you silly."

"You won't slap anybody," I said. "Not as long as I'm around."

He pawed his face again. "What're you going to do?"

"What do you think I'm going to do?"

"You can't turn us in. You don't have any proof . . . it's your word against ours."

"Wrong again." I showed him the voice-activated recorder I'd had hidden in my pocket the entire evening. High-tech, state-of-the-art equipment, courtesy of George Agonistes, fellow investigator and electronics genius. "Everything that was said in your office and in this room tonight is on tape. I've also got the cassette tape Annette played when she called your office number. Voice prints will prove you were talking to yourself on the phone, giving yourself instructions for the money drop. If your wife wants to press charges, you're looking at jail time. Both of you."

"She won't press charges. Not Carolyn."

"I wouldn't be too sure about that."

"Jay," Byers said, "don't let him walk out of here with our money." A frantic note had come into her voice. "Don't let him."

Cohalan said to me, "I suppose you intend to take it straight back to her."

"No, he's gonna try to keep it for himself. Stop him, for God's sake. Stop him, Jay!"

"Straight back to your wife, that's right," I said. "And if you've got any idea of trying to take it away from her, tonight or any time, get it out of your head. That money's going where you'll never lay hands on it again."

"No," he said. Then, "I *could* take it away from you."

"You think so?"

Byers: "Go ahead, do it!"

Cohalan: "I'm as big as you . . . younger, faster."

That's one of the things that makes crank such a nasty drug. It not only speeds you up, it creates a false sense of power and invincibility. On meth, cowards like Cohalan start to think they're tough guys after all.

I repocketed the recorder. I could have showed him the .38, but I grinned at him instead—the kind of death's-head grin I can work up at times like this. "Go ahead and try," I said.

"I need that money, damn you."

"Go ahead and try."

Sweat made Cohalan's face shiny; his stare seemed to be losing focus, the way eyes do when they're about to cross.

Byers half-screamed, "Well, what're you waiting for? Take it!"

He ignored her. Weighing the odds, wondering if he really was man enough, wondering if he'd loaded his bloodstream with sufficient crank to make him man enough.

"Make your move, Cohalan. Or else step away from the door. You've got five seconds."

He moved in three, as I took a step toward him. Sideways, clear of both me and the door. Not enough drug, too much yellow.

"Bullshitter," Byers spat at him, "pansy-ass!" And in the next second she charged me with her hands hooked into claws, one grabbing for the briefcase, the other slashing red-tipped nails at my face.

Men should not hit women; that's an edict I believe in and live by. But in this case I had no choice. I twisted just in time to avoid being raked and backhanded her across the side of the head. It stopped her, put her enough off balance so that I could follow up with a hard shove. Cohalan caught her on reflex, held her. She fought free of him, glared at me but thought better of another rush. She turned on him instead, called him a name. He called her something worse. She one-upped him and then some; she had a mouth like a sewer rat.

I went out in the middle of it and closed the door against their vicious, whining voices. Bleeders, druggies, fools. Jesus.

Outside, the fog had thickened to a near drizzle, slicking the pavement and turning the lines of parked cars along both curbs into two-dimensional onyx shapes. I walked quickly to California. Nobody had bothered my tired old wheels in the bus zone. I locked the briefcase in the trunk, got rolling, then used the car phone to call Carolyn Dain. It was Dain because like a lot of women these days, Kerry included, she'd preferred to keep her own name after marriage.

She answered on the second ring, and as soon as I identified myself she said, "We were right, weren't we." Flat statement, not a question. "The whole thing was just a . . . scam."

"I'm sorry, Ms. Dain."

"Yes. So am I. Where is he now? Still with her?"

"At her apartment. Both high on methamphetamine. Did you know he was a user?"

"I knew," she admitted. "It's been going on for a long time, as long as . . . the other women. I should have told you."

"Yes, you should have." Not that it had taken me long to figure it out on my own. "I put a scare into them and I don't think he'll bother you tonight. But you'd be wise to spend the night someplace else."

"I've already made arrangements."

"Okay, good. Are you going to press charges?"

"I. . . . don't know yet."

"Well, if you don't do it immediately, I'd advise you to stay away from your husband so he can't influence you in any way. And also not to waste any time putting the money into a safe deposit box or a bank account in your name only."

"Yes, all right."

"I have the cash with me, the full seventy-five thousand. I wouldn't hold out any hope of getting the rest of your inheritance back."

"I don't care about that right now."

"I can bring the money out to you. Or meet you wherever you'll be staying. . . ."

"I mean I don't care about *any* of the money right now," she said. "Please don't be offended, but I don't want to see anyone tonight except the person I'm staying with. You can understand that, I'm sure."

"Yes, ma'am, but seventy-five thousand dollars is a lot of money. I don't like being responsible for it."

"You're bonded. I trust you."

"Still, I'd prefer to—"

"Don't you have someplace safe to keep it? Just for tonight?"

"I suppose so, but. . . ."

"Please. Just for tonight. I can't . . . I simply can't cope with any more of this. Please."

"If you insist," I said reluctantly. "I'll keep it until tomorrow, but you'll have to take possession as soon as possible."

"Yes, thank you."

"Let me have the address and phone number of where—"

"I'll call you at your office," she said, and the line went dead.

Well, hell. Shaken up, the underpinnings of her life torn loose. . . . who could blame her for needing time and space, giving short shrift to the money? It was the root cause of all this. And she didn't much care about financial matters anyway, except to provide the basics; she'd told me that the day I took her on as a client. Music was what she cared about. She taught music appreciation and the history of classical music at White Rock School, one of the city's private high schools. Played the flute "passably well" and was gathering data for a "probably-never-to-be-written" biography of an Austrian musicographer named Ludwig Köchel, who had cataloged all of Mozart's compositions in chronological order. What a woman with her taste and interests was doing married to a sorry-ass specimen like Jay Cohalan was anybody's guess.

I turned the car around and drove downtown to my office on O'Farrell. The neighborhood, on the westward fringe of the Tenderloin, is not the safest at eleven o'clock, despite some upscaling in recent years: a heavy influx of Vietnamese and Cambodian families and the reclamation of the nearby Sgt. John Macaulay Park, once a notorious drug gallery and open-air toilet, now a children-only playground. Still, crack dealers, homeless alcoholics, and recent parolees roamed the area at night, and it pays to be vigilant. Fortunately there was a parking space a couple of doors from my building. I made sure I had the immediate vicinity to myself before I unlocked the trunk and hauled the briefcase out.

The building is a tomb at this hour. Nobody in either of the other two businesses that occupy it—Bay City Realtors on the ground floor, the Slim-Taper Shirt Company on the second floor—stays on the premises past 5:30. There'd been a brace of break-ins a few years back, though in neither case had anything been stolen from my top-floor office, probably because that was in the days before I'd hired Tamara to computerize the operation, and there hadn't been much there worth stealing. Pressure on the owner had led to better security measures, and we hadn't had any trouble since.

I rode the tiny, creaking elevator to the third floor, keyed myself in, put on a light, and went straight to the coat closet. That's where the office safe is, bolted to the floor in one corner. It's an old Mosler that anybody with a minimum of safecracking skills could have open in twenty minutes, but since I seldom keep anything of value inside, I'd never seen a need to pay for an upgrade. Carolyn Dain's money ought to be secure enough overnight, given the fact that no one but me knew its whereabouts.

The briefcase was too bulky to fit into the safe, so I unpacked the stacks of bills and stored them in neat rows. It was an odd feeling, handling that much cash—as if I were doing something that was not quite wholesome. Maybe it had to do with all the people I'd encountered in thirty-some years as a cop and private investigator, all the scheming and violence and suffering I'd seen in quests for stacks of bills like these. Filthy lucre. Blood money. Cold, hard cash. Throwaway terms that had deeper, much more bitter meanings for men and women like me.

When I was done, I made sure the safe was locked, slid the empty case into the kneehole of my desk, locked up, and went home to a far better pair of human beings than I'd dealt with so far on this cold early-winter night.

4

KERRY WAS STILL AWAKE, IN BED READING. "I couldn't get to sleep," she said when I came in.

"Worried about me?"

"Always. How did it go?"

"Fine. I miscalculated on one point, but it worked out all right." I'd kept her apprised of what was happening with the Dain case, the little sting I'd planned for tonight. "Most damn satisfying job I've had in a while."

"So you nailed Cohalan and his bimbo."

"Real good."

"Is your client going to press charges?"

"She doesn't know yet. She didn't want to see me tonight, not even to take possession of her money. Too upset."

"You mean you still have all that cash?"

"In the office safe until tomorrow."

She ran her fingers through her already touseled auburn hair. She'd had it cut short recently; the new style fit her pretty well, and she thought it made her look younger, but I hadn't gotten used to it yet. I still preferred the old, longer style.

"Well, I'm glad you didn't bring it home," she said. "I wouldn't feel comfortable with that much much money in the house."

"That's why I put it in the safe."

"What was the one miscalculation?"

I told her about that while I shed my coat and tie and shirt.

"It wouldn't have been your fault if Byers had hit somebody," Kerry said.

"Morally it would have. I didn't need to play Cohalan's game. I could've picked up the money myself after he made the drop, then gone to confront them."

"More effective the way you handled it."

"More dramatic anyway. Looking for a little drama and excitement to spice up my mundane life."

"Thanks a bunch."

"I meant my professional life." I reached over and patted one of the curves outlined by the bedclothes. "I've got all the personal drama and excitement I can handle right here."

"Uh-huh. Sweet talk doesn't feed the bulldog, mister."

"What's that supposed to mean?"

"I don't have a clue. I heard somebody say it in a meeting the other day . . . you know how advertising people talk. I like the way it sounds, even if it doesn't make much sense."

I struggled out of my shoes and socks, massaged one foot and then the other; my feet have a tendency to swell when I do a lot of sitting around. "Emily okay? I was going to look in on her, but I didn't want to chance waking her up."

"I talked her into playing a couple of games of Scrabble before she went to sleep," Kerry said. "She seemed to enjoy that. But she's still so quiet and withdrawn . . . it hurts me to see her like that."

"Me, too. I've been thinking that I need to make more time for her."

"So have I. The same thing."

"Well, I've got tomorrow afternoon free. I thought maybe I'd take her to the zoo or the aquarium after school, just the two of us."

"She'd love that. You know she idolizes you."

"I don't want to be idolized. Too much responsibility."

"I idolize you."

"Sweet talk doesn't feed the bulldog, lady."

She laughed. "How about the three of us doing something together on the weekend, both days? We could take Emily up to the Delta— I haven't been to the Delta in years, and I don't know that she's ever been there. I'm supposed to attend a conference Saturday morning, but she's more important. The agency won't lose any business just because I'm not there to offer my usual brilliant suggestions."

"That's a plan, then."

"And we don't let anything prevent us from following through. Pact?"

"Pact."

I pulled on my pajama bottoms and got into bed. Kerry had her book fanned open on her belly, a slender trade paperback with a picture of what looked like an Egyptian sarcophagus on the front cover. The title was *Forever Lasting;* there was a subtitle to go with it, but I couldn't make it out.

"What's that you're reading?"

"A book Paula loaned me."

"Paula Hanley?"

"Do we know any other Paulas?"

"Oh, God," I said. "Lady Crackpot."

"She is not a crackpot."

"No? That woman's pot is so cracked you couldn't fix it with a kilo of Crazy Glue."

She let me hear one of her little warning growls. "This book," she said, "is actually very interesting. It's all about—"

"I don't want to hear what it's all about."

"That's the trouble with you. You have a closed mind sometimes."

"Where Paula and her ideas are concerned, that's right. Closed in self-defense."

"*Forever Lasting* is not only a fascinating history, it offers a whole new—"

"I said I don't want to hear it. Turn out the light."

"No. I'm going to read a while longer."

I slid my hand over onto her bare thigh.

Pretty soon she said, "Well, maybe I won't read any more tonight," and turned out the light.

Everybody has some sort of curse in his life, large or small. Mine is Kerry's friend, Paula Hanley. Paula is one of San Francisco's highest paid interior decorators. An article Kerry showed me in one of those *Beautiful Homes* magazines said she had "exquisite taste." Maybe so, where her business was concerned, but she dresses like a Technicolor nightmare; whenever I see her I have an urge to put on very dark sunglasses. She bickered incessantly with her rabbity chiropractor husband, drank too much, prosletyzed too much on any subject of interest to her, and worst of all, she was a magnet for and a repository of Weird with a capital W. Fads and fancies were her specialty. She'd been into Esalen, primal scream therapy, channeling and past life regression, rolfing, tantric sex, acupuncture, and a great many others I'd mercifully forgotten about. Whatever this lastest folly, contained in that ominous little book titled *Forever Lasting*, I wanted nothing to do with in any way, shape, or form.

So naturally Kerry had to tell me all about it over breakfast. I tried to stop her, but she has a blind spot where La Hanley is concerned; she seldom buys into Paula's Weird, but she does listen to it and think about it and every now and then one of these wacko concepts strikes a responsive chord in her. I live in mild dread of those times—and it looked and sounded as though this was one of them. As she explained in chilling detail the screwball concept of *Forever Lasting*, her cheeks took on a faint flush, and her eyes got bright and just a bit dreamy. And I sat there with my appetite waning and all sorts of impure thoughts about Paula Hanley dancing in my head.

When Kerry was done explaining, she said, "Now really, isn't that interesting? What do you think?"

If I'd answered that question truthfully, she might have decided to divorce me. I was trying to think of a tactful, noncommittal answer when Emily walked into the dining room. Little pitchers, by God. I said to Kerry, "We'll talk about it later," and she nodded. Even a short reprieve is better than no reprieve at all.

Emily was dressed in the uniform white blouse and dark skirt they make the kids wear in her private school. She hated the outfit, that was plain, but she'd made no more than a token complaint about it. All her complaints were token: briefly expressed and seldom repeated. That was another thing that made communication with her difficult. If she'd gotten angry now and then, thrown a tantrum like most other ten year olds, we'd have had a better psychological understanding of her. But she guarded her emotions, kept them locked away inside; faint glimpses, like subliminal messages, were all you ever got to see of them.

Part of it was genetic; part of it was learned behavior. She was her mother's child in too many ways. Shiela Hunter had been closed-off, secretive, self-involved, fear-ridden—anything but a nurturing parent. She and Emily's father, Jack Hunter, had structured their lives and Emily's life as a tightly knit, rigidly controlled unit, permitting only superficial relationships with others. They'd done it for selfish reasons, because they were afraid of their past transgressions catching up with them, and with no thought to the effects this would have on their daughter. Two separate, bitter tragedies had destroyed the closed unit and left Emily more alone than ever. She seemed on the surface to have handled the loss of her parents as well as any child could; she was a strong, resilient, and very intelligent little girl. But on the inside? That was what worried us, that and the long-range effects. She looked like her mother, the same dark-haired, luminous-eyed, willowy beauty; suppose she grew up to be like her mother—closed-off, secretive, self-involved, fear-ridden?

This morning she was her usual quiet, polite self, until I asked her if she'd like to spend the afternoon at the zoo. Then she perked up some.

The prospect of the three of us spending the weekend together brightened her smile even more. The one thing Kerry and I had no doubt about was that Emily liked and trusted us, wanted to be with us. It was not only because we were surrogate parents; she seemed to genuinely care for us as individuals. The source of worry here was that she viewed and would keep on viewing the relationship as the same kind of tightly knit unit she'd had with her natural parents. Kerry and I had leanings in that direction; neither of us had a lot of friends or outside interests. Had Emily sensed that in us, responded to us in part for that reason? And if she had, what could we do about it?

Whenever possible we took turns driving Emily to her school in Glen Park. My turn today. When I dropped her off I said, "Your last class ends at one-thirty, right?"

"One-forty."

"One-forty. I'll be here waiting."

She said seriously, "If something comes up and you can't make it, I'll understand. Really."

"Listen, kiddo, nothing is going to keep us from going to the zoo this afternoon. This is our day together. Okay?"

"Okay."

Sometimes, when I drop her off, she leans over and gives me a peck on the cheek; other times she just gets out and lifts her hand in a little wave. Today she smiled, one of her rare smiles without a trace of wistfulness or sadness, and shyly touched my hand. Somehow that smile and that touch made me feel better than any of those dutiful little kisses or waves.

Everything was fine at the office. Carolyn Dain's seventy-five thousand was still neatly stacked inside the safe—not that I'd been concerned about it, particularly, but caretaking other people's money always makes me uneasy. After I checked the safe, I went to see if there was a message from the rightful owner. No message. No messages at all, in fact. I thought about ringing up her house, but it was still early, and she may not have returned from wherever she'd spent the night. There was also a chance Cohalan had gone home last night rather than shack up with his viper-tongued girl-friend, and I had no interest in talking to him this morning.

I made the coffee and was pouring a cup when Tamara came in. I couldn't help a small double-take. Clothes had never been her long suit—no pun intended. Her outfits when I'd first hired her had consisted of such as orchid-colored slacks, green sandals that showed off a variety of toe rings, men's baggy shirts, and tie-dyed scarves. The grunge look, she called it, and in my experience the only person who dressed more flamboyantly and with less taste was Paula Hanley. Since then Tamara had modified her appearance somewhat, actually wearing shoes and now and then a skirt to the office. Conservative, however, was not a word in her lexicon . . . until today. Today, by God, she was dressed in a light tan suit, a pale blue blouse that set off her dark skin, short-heeled shoes, either nylons or panty-hose, and lipstick that was neither blood-red nor purple.

She caught me staring and scowled. "Don't ask," she said.

"You clean up nice."

"Hah."

"Funeral, wedding, or job interview?"

"Hah."

"Just tell me it's not a job interview."

"Horace," she said.

"What about Horace?" He was her live-in boyfriend, a 250-pound cellist with linebacker eyes.

"His idea. He thinks I need to upgrade my image."

"Any particular reason?"

"I work in a business office, the man says. I want to open my own business someday, the man says. I better start dressing like a busi-nesswoman, the man says."

"The man has a point."

"Besides, it's the Year of the Suit. That's what he says *Vogue* mag-azine says."

"Horace reads *Vogue?*"

She rolled her eyes. "So he bought me this outfit," she said, scowling again. "Some outfit."

"Back in the eighties they called it a Power Suit."

"Yeah—White Power. I feel like Nancy Reagan in black face, you know what I'm sayin'?"

"You don't look like Nancy Reagan, thank God."

"Yeah, well."

"There's nothing wrong with dressing up. Lots of people do it, young African American women included. Or hadn't you noticed?"

"You sound like Horace."

"Is that bad? I'll say it again: You clean up nice."

The compliment pleased her, but she was not in a mood to admit it. "Damn pantyhose pinches my crotch," she said.

No man of my generation is capable of an adequate response to a statement like that. So I said, "Have some coffee, Ms. Corbin, and let's get to work."

We had a couple of cases working in addition to the Dain matter. One was an investigation for an insurance outfit that had good cause to suspect fraud on a personal injury claim; the other was a domestic affairs case involving the custody of two pre-school children. The custody thing was nasty, with allegations of abuse on one side and neglect and drug use on the other. We were looking into the abuse angle for the plaintiff's attorney, and so far it appeared to be unfounded. Which made the work a little less unpleasant.

Tamara tapped away on her new Mac computer, and I made some phone calls and wrote out a report on the domestic affairs investigation, and most of the morning disappeared. The phone rang twice, but neither caller was Carolyn Dain. A little after eleven, I rang up her home number, got her machine and Cohalan's recorded voice. Then I tried White Rock School and was told she was "out for the day," which probably meant she'd called in with some excuse. There was nothing else I could do except keep on waiting. Sooner or later she'd decide it was time to claim her money.

These and other thoughts ran around inside my head, as often happens when I have some down time. The one I was dwelling on when Tamara shut off her computer and stood up to stretch led me to open my mouth.

"Mummies," I said.

"Say what?"

"Mummies. The basic concept—"

"Yeah. Retro, but still cool."

"Oh, so you know about it."

"Sure, I saw it."

"The book?"

"The movie."

"There's a movie too?"

"Brendan Fraser, Arnold what's-his-name. *The Mummy.*"

"What mummy?"

"That's the title, right?"

"The book's title is *Forever Lasting.*"

"I didn't know there was a book."

"You just said you knew about it."

"The movie. I saw the movie."

"The Mummy?"

"Right."

" . . . You don't mean the Karloff movie?"

"Karloff?"

"Boris Karloff. *The Mummy.*"

"Arnold what's-his-name played the mummy."

"No, it was Karloff."

"Vosloo, that's it. Arnold Vosloo."

"Who's Arnold Vosloo?"

"The mummy. Real hunk, for a dead guy."

"What does Arnold Vosloo have to do with *Forever Lasting?* For that matter what does Karloff have to do with it?"

"What's *Forever Lasting?*"

"The book about mummies!"

She looked at me. I looked at her. Pretty soon she said, "What're we talking about here?"

"Mummies. I asked you about mummies, not movies."

"*The Mummy* is a movie."

I opened my mouth and then shut it again. It was like being trapped in the middle of an Abbott and Costello routine, but I didn't say so; if I had, Tamara would probably have said, "Who're Abbott and Costello?" and we'd have been off again on another round. Sometimes the generation gap is a chasm as wide as the Grand Canyon.

I took a few seconds to make a careful selection of materials before I attempted to build another bridge. "What I'm trying to ask you," I said, "is your opinion of mummification. The concept of mummifying dead bodies instead of burying or incinerating them."

"Oh," she said. "Egyptian history. Cleopatra, King Tut."

"Yes and no. There's plenty of history in *Forever Lasting,* so I'm told, but it all leads to present-day funeral practices and a pitch for the so-called art of commercial mummification."

"They still do that? Embalm dead folks and make mummies out of them?"

"Evidently. Seems to be more than one company specializing in modern mummification. And this Forever Lasting outfit is doing well enough to print up an entire book about it."

"Man," she said.

"Yeah," I said.

"So what do they do? Use bandages and stuff like the Egyptians?"

"Oh, they're a lot more sophisticated than that. They drop the body into some chemical brew for a few days, formaldehyde and salt and God knows what else, and when it's all dried out they treat it with scented oils and then bind it in linen topped with polyurethane so the cloth won't deteriorate."

"Then what? Don't be telling me they seal it up in a sarcophagus?"

"Just what they do. Only they call it a mummiform. You can get one made out of bronze that resembles King Tut's. Or made out of silver or gold, and crusted with jewels. You can even get an art deco coffin, any design—engraved likeness of yourself or your family members, even."

"Dag," she said.

"Yeah," I said.

"Where do they put the mummies afterward?"

"Private crypts and mausoleums. Or you can buy a niche in Forever Lasting's Chamber of Eternal Rest."

"What's that?"

"The guy who runs this outfit, Joseph Im-tep—"

"Joseph *what?*"

"Im-tep. Real name Joseph Schultz, but he took an Egyptian name when he founded Forever Lasting."

" . . . You making that up."

"Do I sound like I'm kidding here?"

"Joseph Im-tep. Wonder why he bothered to leave out the 'ho'?"

"What 'ho'?" I said, which made me sound like an Englishman on a fox hunt.

"You know, Im-*ho*-tep. Mummy's name in the movie."

"Let's not get started on that again. This Im-tep guy owns some property in the Sangre de Cristo Mountains in New Mexico, claims to have his Chamber of Eternal Rest built inside a cave up there— niches carved into the rock where the mummified bodies can quote enjoy blissful solitude for all eternity unquote."

"What's all this cost?"

"Well, let's see. You can get your dead body mummified without any of the trappings for under ten thousand."

"Dollars?"

"Dollars. If you want a funeral and flowers and one of the cheaper airtight coffins, the tab'll run you around twenty-five thousand. The fancy gold-and-silver mummiforms cost a hundred and fifty grand or so. And if you want a niche in the Chamber of Eternal Rest, that's another seventy-five hundred."

"Off da hook!" she said.

"Yeah," I said.

"And rich people actually go for this?"

"Rich and not so rich. A lot more than you'd think."

"What's the big attraction?"

"Im-tep's selling it as a kind of immortality. Mummifed bodies last forever, at least in theory."

"Yeah, forever. If some dude with an archeology degree or a handful of tanna leaves doesn't show up." Tamara came over and perched a plump hip on the edge of my desk. "No way you be thinking about turning yourself into King Tut?"

"Me? Good God, no."

"So how come you read this *Forever Lasting* book?"

"I didn't read it. Kerry's reading it."

"*She's* not? . . ."

"Just finds the subject interesting, she says. I'd divorce her if she let Paula Hanley talk her into contacting Im-tep, and she knows it. Paula's the one who loaned her the book."

"So that girl's serious about getting mummified?"

"She is now. In the unlikely event she stays serious, she'll probably want to design her own mummiform." I had a mental image of a golden sarcophagus, elegantly and tastefully carved—and inside it, Mrs. Boris Karloff resplendant in linen bindings of shocking pink and bilious green, Day-Glo orange and fetching lavender.

"But you don't think it'll happen?"

"I'll be astonished if it does. By next week or next month, Paula will be into something else—burial at sea decked out in United Nations flags, maybe. She's not too well wrapped."

Tamara laughed.

"What's funny?"

"Pun you just made."

"What pun?"

"'Not too well wrapped.' Neither was Im-ho-tep."

I frowned. "You know I don't like puns."

"Well, it came out your mouth."

"Unintentionally."

"Right. You a man who doesn't make puns on purpose, doesn't even get 'em half the time." She stood up and smoothed her new skirt. "You really want my opinion on this mummy business?"

"That's why I brought it up."

"Truth is, it leaves me cold."

"I'm glad to hear it. Me, too."

"How about we lay it to rest now? We done talked the subject to death."

"Fine with me."

She favored me with one of her funny little smiles. "Well then," she said, "I guess that's a wrap," and went back to her desk and sat there chuckling to herself.

As much as I like Tamara, she can be strange sometimes. Not quite but almost as strange as Paula Hanley.

5

IT WAS CROWDED AT THE SAN FRANCISCO Zoological Gardens. Nonstormy Fridays are usually busy days, even at this time of year. Overcast, fog, and icy winds don't keep visitors away; if they did, the zoo would go out of business inside a year. Its seventy-some acres are spread out so close to the ocean you can hear breakers lashing the seawall across the Great Highway which forms the zoo's western boundary. Most days out here, you get a brisk sea wind; most days the afternoons are chilly even when the sky is stripped clean of clouds or mist. This one was no exception. Patchy sun and cloud scuds, but offshore a huge fogbank was getting ready to unroll again like a giant fuzzy carpet, and the wind blew sharp and cold. I had my overcoat and gloves on, and Emily was bundled into a heavy wool coat, mittens, scarf, and knitted cap, but neither of us minded the cold or the bulky outfits. She was smiling, and there was a skip in her step, both very good to see.

The zoological gardens have expanded quite a bit since a financier named Herbert Fleishhacker contributed enough money and animals to open them in the early 1920s. Back then, and for some time afterward, they had been small and modest and known as Fleishhacker Zoo. Next door had been Fleishhacker's Pool, the world's largest outdoor saltwater swimming pool at a thousand feet long and a hundred-and-fifty feet wide, known locally as "Herb's white elephant" since hardly anybody used it because of the weather and Ocean Beach being so close by. When the pool was finally shut down, the zoo took over the land and a lot more animals and exhibits were added. Today it's one of the largest on the West Coast, with fourteen hundred animals and birds and dozens of grottoes, brushy fields and slopes, rush-rimmed ponds, and other areas simulating natural habitats.

If you want to see everything the zoo has to offer, you need a full day to prowl those seventy acres. In the three hours we had, the choices were somewhat limited. Emily was interested in birds, so the big aviary was a definite stop. So were Monkey Island and the Primate Discovery Center, the sea lion tank, the koala compound, and the Lion House.

We went to the aviary first, then wandered over to see if it was feeding time for the big cats. It wasn't; all but one of the cages was empty, the animals still out back in their grottoes. We stopped in front of the occupied cage, where one of the Bengal tigers was pacing restlessly. We were the only two-legged animals on this side of the bars.

I knew the Lion House, the entire zoo grounds all too well. Several years back I had been hired by the Zoo Commission to investigate a rash of thefts of rare and endangered animals, reptiles, and birds that were being sold off to unscrupulous private collectors. I'd spent three long, cold nights patrolling the grounds in the company of two other watchmen before the case took an unexpected and violent twist: one of the watchmen was found murdered in a lion cage under bizarre circumstances. That night and the case's resolution were still sharp in my memory.

I don't usually discuss my investigations with anyone other than the principals, Tamara, and Kerry. And there are some cases, some dark byways, that I reserve strictly for myself—the stuff of no one's nightmares but my own. But as Emily and I stood in the Lion House, steps away from the cage where the dead man had lain, I found myself giving the kid a watered down version of that night's events. I'm not sure why. A half-conscious attempt to bond with her, maybe, give her a little more knowledge of who I am and what it is I do.

The impulse was right. She listened raptly, not big-eyed as some girls her age might have been, but with a kind of solemn, analytical interest. When I was done, she asked some thoughtful, adult-type questions that I tried to answer in kind. Then, after a little time, she asked, "Were you afraid? Not when you found that poor man . . . when you were out in the dark all alone?"

"Well, an empty zoo at night is a pretty scary place."

"It wasn't empty, really."

"That's true. All the animals were here, but they were locked in their cages and compounds."

"Animals aren't scary. People are. The dark is."

I said gently, "Are you afraid of the dark, Emily?"

"Sometimes."

"Me, too. Sometimes."

"Of people, too?"

"I have been. I probably will be again."

"People you know? Or just strangers?"

"A few of both."

"I'm scared all the time," she said.

"Scared of what?"

"Everything. Everybody. The dark. Tomorrow."

Calm voice, but threaded with anguish. It made me ache for her.

"I have to sleep with a light on," she said. "I can't stand the dark. I hate it, being afraid all the time . . . I just can't help it."

"You won't always feel that way."

"What if I do? I'm afraid of that, too."

"It won't happen. Kerry and I won't let it happen." It sounded lame and patronizing even in my own ears, but I didn't know what else to say. What can you say? "You don't feel scared when you're with us, do you?"

"Sometimes."

"You know we wouldn't hurt you, or let you be hurt."

"I know. Not that kind of scared."

"What kind then?"

She shook her head.

"Come on, now. What kind?"

"You . . . might not always be here. You might go away."

"I'm not going anywhere. Neither is Kerry."

"My mom and dad didn't think they were, either. But they did. They went away, both of them."

"You're afraid *we* might die?"

"You could," she said. "An accident, like what happened to my dad. And your job . . . I know it's dangerous. Somebody could . . . do something. . . ."

Careful, now. Denial was a lie, and I could not lie to her. No lame, patronizing answer to this, no glib and meaningless reassurances. She'd finally opened up a little, given me a better look at her emotions, introduced me to a couple of her private demons. If I said the wrong thing, she might shut the door again and keep it shut.

I asked her, "Emily, do you believe anyone is ever really safe?"

"I don't know what you mean."

"Yes you do. Think about it. Is anyone safe all the time, every minute of every day? Safe from being hurt in some way, from dying?"

She said, "No," almost immediately.

"That's right. Things can happen, unexpected things, bad things. Some we can prevent, guard against. Others we can't. You understand that, don't you?"

"Yes."

"Thinking about all those bad things isn't going to change what happens. But it'll change *you* if you let it. Pretty soon you won't be thinking about anything else. You won't even want to go out of the house for fear something bad might happen. You'll be afraid all the time, all your life. You'll never feel safe."

I paused, but she didn't say anything. Just looked up at me with those big, sad brown eyes. So I went on with it, taking a little different slant. "When we were in the aviary and you laughed at the way the two macaws were scolding each other . . . did you feel safe then?"

" . . . Yes."

"Why?"

"Because everything's all right here, now. There's nothing to be afraid of in the daytime at the zoo."

"That's part of it, but there's something else, too. You weren't afraid, you felt safe, because you were having a good time. Thinking good thoughts. That's the whole secret to not being afraid—thinking good thoughts."

She said without sarcasm or irony, just making a statement, "Don't worry, be happy. Like in the song."

"Pretty simple philosophy, I know, but it's true and it works. You believe it?"

"I don't know." Too smart, too introspective, too deeply scarred for any quick and easy fix. But willing to listen, willing to consider the possible validity of adult wisdom. "I want to, but . . . I don't know."

"Give it some thought later on," I said. "Right now, we can either stand here and talk some more about being scared and people dying, or we can go get a soda and a hot dog and then check out the koalas and the monkeys and feed the sea lions. Your choice."

She produced a shy little smile and took my hand. "I am kind of hungry."

"So am I. You like sauerkraut on your hot dog?"

"Ugh," she said.

"Okay, then, we'll load up with mustard instead."

Things were fine again after that. She ate all of her hot dog, drank all of her Diet 7-Up. In the Primate Center some of the monkeys and apes were like stand-up comics, mugging furiously for the onlookers and performing any number of outrageous antics designed to hold center stage; one baboon in particular had both of us laughing out loud. Like everybody, she thought the koalas were cute and cuddly and wished she could hold one. Feeding the sea lions seemed to please her most of all. We stayed for the whole show, and she went through four packages of chopped-up fish. She might've been making a determined effort to enjoy herself, to please me, but if so it was a seamless act. Her pleasure seemed genuine.

It was nearly five when we left the zoo grounds. The fog had rolled in, and the temperature had dropped several more degrees as night approached. In the car I put the heater on first thing, and while it was warming up and Emily and I were thawing out, I checked in with Tamara.

"Carolyn Dain called twice," she said. "I tried to call *you* three times."

The note of exasperation in her voice said I was in for another communications lecture. Tamara had been trying to talk me into carrying a cell phone, or at least a pager or one of those little hand-held message computers; she kept insisting that a car phone wasn't enough, that I was out of touch too often while away from the office. Maybe she was right. But to my old-fashioned, technophobic way of thinking, there were too many electronic gadgets in the world and I did not care to get involved with any more than the necessary minimum. I don't believe people should be ringing and beeping in public places. And I especially don't believe in the modern rite of invading others' space and privacy by engaging in loud, one-sided conversations, business or personal, thereby foolishly calling attention to yourself the way the monkeys in the Primate Center had done. There's too damn little common courtesy these days, without me adding to the general decline.

To forestall Tamara's lecture, I said quickly, "Did you tell her she could come in and pick up her money?"

"I told her."

"And?"

"She wants you to deliver it. Sounded kind of upset, second time she called."

"Upset?"

"You know, nervous, like something was bothering her."

"Her husband, maybe. Is she home now?"

"Said she was. Wanted me to bring the money out to her, but I told her that wasn't my job. This girl don't make no house calls with bags full of cash."

"You're right, it's my job. Okay, I'll swing in now and pick up the money and deliver it. If she calls again, tell her I'm on my way."

"Want me to wait til you get here?"

"No need. Go ahead and lock up when you're ready."

I would have preferred to drop Emily off at the condo, but when I called I got the machine and then remembered that Kerry'd said she might have to work late tonight. Emily said she didn't mind going with me. In fact, the prospect seemed to please her—a way to prolong our day together.

So we drove downtown and I took her upstairs to the office. She'd been there once before—I felt she ought to see where I conducted the business part of my life—and she hadn't seemed particularly impressed. You couldn't blame her. It was a big, old-fashioned loft, once an artist's studio, with a high ceiling, nondescript decor, a couple of windows that offered an impressive view of the ass-end of the federal building downhill, and a suspended light fixture that looked like a grappling hook surrounded by clusters of brass testicles. Emily had grown up in a deliberately shelted environment in Greenwood, an affluent community down the Peninsula; this was a whole new world to her.

Tamara was gone, so we had the place to ourselves. While I opened the safe, Emily fetched Cohalan's briefcase from under my desk. Then she stood quietly watching as I transferred the stacks of currency.

When I was done she said, "Why do people think money is so important?"

"Not everybody does. Just some people."

"Like my mom and dad."

I was not about to go there with her. "They think that if you have enough of it, you can buy all the things you want and it'll solve all your problems. But they're wrong. What they don't realize is that money can only change the outside of you. You're still the same person inside, rich or poor, good or bad."

She nodded. "I don't want a lot of money when I get older."

I didn't ask her what she did want because I was pretty sure I knew—the basics, anyway. She wanted stability and the illusion of safety. She wanted people she cared about not to die suddenly. She wanted to be noticed and nurtured and allowed to grow up to be her own person. She wanted not to be hurt any more. She wanted to be loved.

But I would not go there with her, either. Not verbally. Actions were what counted, not words. So I said, "That's a good attitude to have," and smiled at her and let it go at that.

Daly City was gray and wet with fog and black with early night. When the beachfront stables of the San Francisco Riding Academy loomed spectrally ahead, I slowed and made the first inland turn off Skyline. It occurred to me as I did that Emily might like to take lessons at the academy, since she'd been enrolled at one of the exclusive stables in horsy Greenwood. I asked her, and she said, "Well, maybe." She didn't sound particularly enthusiastic. Could be riding was a pursuit Sheila or Jack Hunter had pressed on her in their desire to fit in with Greenwood's elite. I wouldn't make the same mistake. If Emily decided she wanted to join the academy here, the decision would be entirely hers.

Carolyn Dain and Jay Cohalan lived in a modest tract home a couple of streets to the east. I found the place and pulled up in front. The house was painted a yellow color that had a faint greenish tinge in the fog; the only other thing that distinguished it from the lines of single-family dwellings in the neighborhood was a row of cypress shrubs that had been trimmed into topiary shapes in the narrow front yard. The driveway was empty, but light shone behind drawn drapes in the picture window.

Emily asked, "Can I come with you?"

"Better if you wait here. I won't be long."

She said, "Okay," and settled down with her hands folded in her lap. She was good at waiting, being by herself. She'd had plenty of practice when her selfish, fearful parents had been alive.

I got the briefcase from the trunk, hurried through the windy drizzle of fog. The doorbell made a discordant noise inside, as if there was something wrong with the chiming mechanism. Almost immediately the door opened inward. I said, "Ms. Dain?" because I couldn't see her behind it, and at the same time took a couple of steps into a dim hallway lit only by a spill of lampglow from the living room.

As soon as I cleared the far edge, my head swiveling to look around the door, it came swinging past me with enough force to create a swishing sound. I heard it slam, saw a dark shape moving—registered man, not woman—and in the next instant something slammed across the side of my neck and jaw. Slash of pain, flare like lightning behind my eyes, and I was off balance, stumbling, throwing an arm up as the shape crowded in on me. Grunt, his or mine. A downsweeping blur—

This time the blow glanced off my upraised elbow, cracked hard across my ear, knocked me down in a roaring confusion of heat and sparks and black-streaked hurt.

6

I DID NOT LOSE CONSCIOUSNESS EVEN FOR A second, but I was cockeyed and disoriented, trying to crawl and get up at the same time. I heard and felt him scrabbling above me, the onion-laden hiss and pant of his breath. He tore the briefcase out of my grasp. I tried to fight him, but my body wouldn't obey the command; the only motor responses it seemed capable of in those first few seconds were crawling and struggling to rise.

My head bumped into something, *wall*, and just as that happened, his weight came down hard on my back, crushed me flat to the floor. I heard myself gasping and choking for air. A knee bored between my shoulder blades, something hard jabbed the nape of my neck. Words filtered through the addled haze, the noise I was making: "Lay still, you old fuck." I'd been squirming; I quit that, not because he'd told me to but because my wind and strength were starting to come back. The object moved higher on my neck, to the bone above my left ear. Steadied there, digging into skin and hair. I knew what it was then: the muzzle of a short-barreled revolver.

"All right," he said.

Clicking sound, soft and yet as loud as an explosion—the hammer being thumbed back to cock.

He's going to kill me!

Terror mushroomed. My body surged in a wild effort to twist, turn, roll away, get my hands up.

He squeezed the trigger.

The hammer fell, I heard or thought I heard the click as it fell. Then I heard him say "Shit!" because nothing had happened, the gun hadn't fired, it must have jammed jammed jammed—

There was a great, savage tearing sensation inside me, as if I were ripped apart and put back together whole all at once. Fury consumed terror, burned the haze out of my mind. I heaved up, bellowing like an animal, and pitched him off to one side. Flopped half around so I could see him through a smear of blood and pain—big, dark, thick bushy eyebrows, bald on top, nobody I'd ever seen before.

He clubbed at me with the useless gun, missed, connected glancingly off my shoulder as I lunged up from the waist. I clawed at his face, dug in nails, ripped a deep furrow in his cheek. He made a screeching noise, missed me again with a reflexive swipe. By then I was on my knees, still bellowing, my hands like pincers groping for his throat. Rage-crazy, all reason flayed out of me . . . if I'd succeeded in getting him by the throat I think I might have kept on squeezing until his face and tongue were swollen black and he was as dead as he'd tried to make me.

But he got that goddamn gun in under my clutching fingers and kicked it up against my jaw, solidly enough to snap my head back, leave me exposed. A second direct jolt drove me backward into the wall, scrambled my head again. If he'd followed up he might have been able to finish what he'd started, only he didn't realize it. He'd had enough of me, enough hurt of his own. And the money was all he really cared about anyway. I heard more than saw him stagger to his feet, stumble over something, regain his balance, and lurch out of there with the briefcase.

As much as I hungered to chase after him, my body would not

permit it. Too much abuse and my supply of adrenaline used up. I knelt there with my head hanging, shaking it, spraying droplets of blood. The door was open; the cold, moist night air started me shivering. I rubbed wet out of my eyes, found that I was in the living room doorway. It took a little time, seconds, minutes, to gather my feet under me and haul myself upright along the jamb. The rage had ebbed some. Now my head was clearing and I could think again . . .

Emily!

The wildness came rushing back. I shoved off the wall, took two or three rubber-legged steps toward the door.

And she was there, Emily, materializing phantom-like out of the foggy dark. I had to blink and stare to be sure I was really seeing her. She was running, but her steps faltered as she came inside; one hand splayed up against her mouth. "Daddy! Oh, God, you're hurt!"

I stood swaying, weak again, draining again. If she hadn't caught hold of my arm and steadied me, I might've gone down. Little girl, thin, weighed no more than ninety pounds, but she had surprising strength—adult strength.

"Daddy, you're bleeding. . . ."

The first time she'd called me Daddy, it hadn't really penetrated; this time it did, made me want to grab her and hug her close. Made me want to cry. Why it affected me that way, given the condition I was in, I don't know. Maybe because it revealed just how deeply her feelings for me ran.

"Not as bad as it looks," I said. The words had a liquidy sound, as if they were bleeding too.

"Should I call nine-eleven?"

"No, nobody yet. Let me sit down for a minute."

She helped me into the living room, to a chair in there. I was able to lean on her a little, another measure of her strength. In the lamplight I could see the blood on my hands and the front of my coat; more wetness trickled down into the collar of my shirt. My jaw ached in two or three places and my ear had a cauliflowered feel. I explored gingerly with the tips of two fingers. Half a dozen cuts and abrasions, all more or less superficial.

When I glanced up, Emily was gone. I called her name; she answered from a distance. Then she was back with a dripping dish-towel from the kitchen. She swabbed gently at my face and neck, turning the towel red. Her face was pale, strained, the big luminous eyes wide and moist.

"I'm okay," I said.

"Are you sure? You don't look very good."

"I don't feel so good, either."

"A doctor? . . ."

"I don't need one. I'll be all right."

"But your head . . . you might need stitches. . . ."

"Emily, did you see the man who ran out of here?"

She bit her lip before she said, "Yes."

"Did he see you?"

"No. He wasn't looking at the car and I stayed inside until he was gone."

"Where'd he go?"

"Down the street. A car parked there."

"Could you tell what kind or color?"

"No, it was too dark."

"Can you describe what he looked like?"

She shook her head. "Who was he?"

"I don't know." I heard those clicks in my head again, the revolver's hammer cocking and then falling. *I could be dead right now.* My stomach twisted; I said between my teeth, "But I'm going to find out."

I got slowly to my feet, took a couple of tentative steps. Still shaky, but I could function. Full reaction hadn't set in yet; when it did, I was not going to be worth much for a while. Do what needed to be done now, as fast as possible.

"Emily, I want you to go out and get in the car, lock the doors, and wait for me. Don't open the door for anyone else, no matter who it is. If anybody comes, blow the horn and keep blowing it."

"What're you going to do?"

"Make a couple of calls. I won't be long."

I went with her to the front door, out onto the porch. The street and sidewalks were empty, no one visible anywhere. It seemed that the bald son of a bitch and I had made enough noise to wake up half of Daly City, but sounds become magnified during a skirmish like that. If they'd carried to the nearby houses, the neighbors had chosen to ignore them: the Great Unwritten Code of Noninvolvement. I watched until Emily had locked herself inside the car, her face a white blur pressed close to the window glass. Then I drew back inside and shut and locked the door.

Except for the uneven rhythm of my breathing, the house was still. Too still. The air felt charged. There was nothing to see in the living room; and nothing in the kitchen or Emily would have reacted. One of the bedrooms, then. Or the back porch. Or the garage. I took a tight hold on myself and went looking.

It didn't take long. Second of two bedrooms—the master bedroom, though it was no larger than the other. The bed was a big double, one of those modern four-posters, and Carolyn Dain was lying facedown in the middle of it. I did not have to go any closer than the doorway to know she was dead. Bloody, powder-scorched hole behind her right ear, blood in her pale yellow hair, blood splattered on the sheet under her head. He'd used a pillow to muffle the shot; it lay beside her, black-burned and leaking kapok or whatever they use to stuff cheap pillows nowadays.

Execution. Pushed facedown, knee in the back, gun muzzle pressed tight to the bone above the ear, bang you're dead.

The way I would have died if the revolver hadn't misfired. The way I'd look right now, lying on the hallway floor. My blood. My stillness, that terrible final stillness like no other.

My gorge had risen; I had to swallow half a dozen times to keep the sickness down. The rage had gone cold in me, like a deep-driven wedge of ice. I kept standing there, staring over at the bed. I could not seem to make myself move.

Carolyn Dain. Teacher, music lover, music historian. Average woman with average needs and average feelings, living an average life in an average neighborhood of an average city. Human being. Victim. Dead before her fortieth birthday on account of a philandering, corrupt husband and a cold-blooded, merciless thief. And sure to be too little mourned, too soon forgotten.

Seventy-five thousand dollars. She'd been killed for nothing more than that; I had almost died for nothing more than that. Two human beings—sacrifices on a subhuman's altar of greed.

I have hated, truly, primitively hated, only a handful of men in my life. The bald man, whoever he was, had joined that select few. I no longer believe in capital punishment, but standing there then, looking at what was left of Carolyn Dain, hearing those hammer clicks again and again in my mind, I yearned to see him as dead as she was, as he'd tried to make me. I ached to dance on his grave.

It might have been a long time, or only a minute or two, before I grew aware of the bedroom itself. It had been thoroughly searched. Drawers pulled out, articles of clothing and other items strewn over the shag carpet, clothing and boxes spilling out of a small walk-in closet. Carolyn Dain's purse was there, too, riffled and emptied. Predator's hunt for more money, jewelry, anything else of value. Before or after he killed her? Depended on whether he'd come here with her or gotten into the house some other way and been waiting when she arrived. Depended on who he was and how he'd found out about the money.

The friend she'd spent the night with? Not likely. Somebody connected to Cohalan or Annette Byers or both of them? Good bet. It seemed out of character for Cohalan to arrange or collude in his wife's murder; but I could see him setting up a robbery to get his hooks on the cash, and not knowing or wanting to know how blood-sick his accomplice was. Byers . . . same thing. Or one or the other of them might have inadvertently tipped Baldy off. Or Carolyn Dain might have in some way, if she'd known him.

Possibilities. I told myself it was up to the cops to explore them, not me. I told myself I was going to be out of it soon enough, and a good thing, too. I told myself I was a lucky survivor, and I'd damn well better let it go at that. And all the while I kept hearing those clicks, the hammer being drawn back to cock, the hammer falling as he squeezed the trigger.

I'd had enough of this room, of the death it contained. I made myself turn away, took a quick look through the rest of the house and then returned to the living room. A desk with a computer on it stood in one corner; I hadn't noticed it before. A couple of the drawers were pulled partway out, and papers littered the surface. He'd been in there, too, hunting for valuables. I started over that way, drawn by the swarm of papers.

The telephone rang.

It brought me up short, the noise scraping at my nerves like the blade of a rasp. I located the thing on a stand beside the desk, listened to it ring twice more. Then there was the sound an answering machine makes when it kicks in, and Jay Cohalan's recorded voice said, "Hello. I am Jay and Carolyn's machine. I am the only one here right now. At the beep tell me who, what, where, when, and why, and I will pass it on as soon as I can. Have a nice day." Just like him, that message. Smart-ass and verbose.

"Carolyn? It's Mel. If you're there, pick up." Male voice, youngish, deep-pitched, with a note of urgency in it. There was a pause, and then: "You were supposed to call me, remember? Give me a buzz as soon as you get this message and let me know if everything's all right. You know how worried I am after last night."

Mel. "How worried I am after last night." Was he the friend she'd gone to spend the night with? Sauce for the goose?

I went ahead to the desk. The one thing you never do, if you're a private investigator who wants to keep his license, is disturb anything at a crime scene. Special circumstances here, though, oh yeah. I pawed through the papers and drawers, doing it carefully, using my handkerchief whenever I touched a surface that would take fingerprints. Bills and receipts, mostly. No personal correspondence. No Rolodex or address book. Nothing with the name Mel on it.

Back to the master bedroom. I kept my eyes off the bed as I picked my way in and squatted where the contents of her purse had been dumped. It took a few seconds to find a thin red leatherette address book under a fold of the bedspread. Fewer than twenty entries in a small, neat hand—pathetically few for a woman in her late thirties. Most seemed to have some connection to White Rock School: teachers, a principal, a vice principal. No relatives, or at least no one named Dain or Cohalan. Initials and surnames only, three of the initials M. I thought about copying those three names and addresses into my notebook, but I was beginning to feel shaky, a little disoriented. Reaction setting in; I'd experienced that sort of thing too often not to recognize the symptoms.

When I straightened, using a bureau corner for support, a wave of vertigo came over me and the rubbery feeling returned to my legs. I leaned against the bureau until the dizziness passed, then groped my way to the living room and collapsed into the desk chair.

Bad now, worse than I could remember. Tingling weakness in my limbs and fingers. Nausea. Pounding in both temples, intensifying the hurt in my ear and jawline. My hearing had gone out of whack—external sounds tuned out, the hammer clicks so clear and loud they might have been happening here and now. I could feel the hard muzzle of the revolver as if it were again . . . still . . . jabbing the bone above my right ear.

Sweat oozed out of me. Blood, too, trickling again from one of the wounds, like a worm crawling on my neck. I still had the wet dish-towel; at some point Emily or I had draped it over my shoulder. My hand trembled as I mopped my face and neck. Panic climbed in me. I fought it down, willing myself calm so I could call the police, call Kerry and have her come and take charge of Emily.

And kept on sitting there, fighting and willing and sweating and shaking, listening to the clicks.

7

THE REST OF THAT NIGHT IS RECORDED IN MY memory as a series of blurred images, disconnected and time warped, like fragments of a film edited and projected by a madman.

Cops in uniforms asking questions that I answered, questions that I couldn't answer.

Kerry, anxious, hovering close by.

Latino police lieutenant named Fuentes, mole on one cheek, humorless half-smile frozen on his mouth. Wanting to know about the money, Carolyn Dain, Cohalan, Annette Byers. Taking the answering machine tape and putting it into a plastic bag. Saying more than once, as if he were making an accusation, "You sure you don't have any idea who the bald man is?"

Paramedics, two of them, male and female, probing my wounds and talking at me and around me. One of them saying, "Head wounds can be tricky, you'd better let us take you to the ER for an X-ray."

Emily, arms tight around my waist, small face upturned, luminous eyes full of wet.

Riding in the ambulance, lights beyond the windows making crazy-quilt patterns on a black backdrop.

Hospital smells, doctors and nurses hurrying, scurrying. Somebody with blood all over him, somebody else moaning and saying over and over, *"Está muerto, Dios Mío, Está muerto."* Machines humming and the touch of cold metal.

Kerry again, telling me in relieved tones that the X-rays were negative, she could take me home now.

Lying next to her in bed, wide awake waiting for some kind of medication to take effect, watching the dark.

And through it all, in every fragment, behind every voice and every sound, I heard the clicks, listened to the clicks—an endless hollow rhythm that matched the beating of my heart.

I was better in the morning. My head ached, there was an odd sort of thrumming in my body like you sometimes have the day after a long plane flight, but otherwise I felt well enough physically. The clicks were muted now, like the faintest of background noises. I told myself I was okay. No head trauma, none of the wounds serious. I was going to be fine. Still alive, still kicking.

I should have been dead.

The click of the hammer cocking should have been the last sound I heard on this earth.

Jammed cartridge, faulty firing pin—pure blind luck. One-in-a-million chance. The gun hadn't misfired for Carolyn Dain, and she was lying dead in the cold room at the morgue. The gun had misfired for me, and here I was moving, thinking, breathing. Alive.

Dead man walking.

I could not drive that thought out of my head. I tried to tell myself that last night's experience was no worse than others I'd lived through. The ordeal in the mountain cabin . . . three months shackled to a wall, three months alone facing my own mortality every minute of every day. The arson fire in the China Basin warehouse, the rigged shotgun at Deep Mountain Lake, too many other close calls. Death was no stranger to me; I'd lived with it in one form or another most of my adult life. And I'd survived. That was what really counted, wasn't it? Survival?

Yes. Right. But this was different somehow.

This was different.

The bore of the revolver tight against the bone above my ear, the click of the hammer cocking, the sudden realization that I was about to take my last breath, live the last second of my life. The helplessness, the fury. And the terror. All of that concentrated into a single instant, intensified a hundredfold. You do not survive a moment like that unchanged in some profound way. Do not simply walk away from it telling yourself you're lucky and then get on with your spared life as if nothing much had happened.

But how had it changed me? In what way was I different this morning than yesterday? I had no answer yet to that question. I felt oddly detached, the way you do in certain dreams, as if part of me was standing off at a distance watching the other part perform the usual daily rituals of showering, shaving, combing hair, getting dressed. I felt calm enough, except for a persistent restlessness. The anger was still there, but it was a faint glow without heat. There was the hate when I thought about the bald man and a desire to see him punished for what he'd done to me and to Carolyn Dain; but they were nothing at all like the consuming hatred and hunger for revenge I'd felt last night or nurtured for so long against the man who had chained me to the cabin wall. No urge to go hunting. No bloodlust. No strong emotion of any kind. Yet it was not as if I were dead inside. Feelings were there but weighted down, smothered. All except one—more of a sensation, really, that had been there when I woke up and that had stayed with me unabated.

I felt as though I were bleeding.

As though the piece that had been torn loose after the gun mis-fired had left an open wound, and the wound was leaking in a slow, steady seepage that would neither cease nor clot. As though a pool of blood were being created deep within, and the weight of that pool was what was smothering my emotions. Irrational notion, but I couldn't shake it. I could not stop the bleeding.

Kerry was Kerry, as always: wife, lover, best friend, buffer zone, and rock in a crisis. She asked if I wanted to talk about what had happened, and I said no, not yet. I didn't want to relive last night even for her, and I had no words to express how I felt. Space was what I needed, separation from everyone for the time being. She'd been through this kind of thing with me before; she understood. She not only left me alone, she got rid of somebody from the media who rang the doorbell and deflected half a dozen callers, including Tamara, my old reporter buddy Joe DeFalco, and Fuentes, the Daly City cop, who wanted my complete file on the Dain-Cohalan case as soon as I could get it to him.

She must have had a talk with Emily, too, because other than a kiss and a hug, I got the same hands-off treatment from her. Only her eyes betrayed her feelings: she was still very frightened and upset. Looking into them, I remembered our little talk yesterday at the zoo, her words *You might not always be here, you might go away,* and my glib philosophical reassurances. And I remembered the way she'd looked when she came running into the Daly City house, and how she'd called me Daddy. I felt badly for her, and angry at myself for not being able to protect her from last night's brand of evil, for putting her in a position where she might also have been a victim. Poor Emily, poor hurt lonely little girl. My little girl now. Yet all the feelings—the empathy, the anger, the sadness, the love—were dulled and superficial at this moment. I was not capable of any strong emotion today, not for anyone including myself.

Daddy, you're bleeding. . . .

The three of us sat quiet at the breakfast table. I drank coffee and made an effort to eat a little of what Kerry put in front of me and couldn't do it. Finally I pushed the plate away. Tried to smile and couldn't manage that, either, as I said, "I don't think I'm up to the Delta trip today."

They both made of-course-not-we-don't-care-about-that sounds. Kerry said, "Why don't you just rest? I'll call Tamara and ask her to take the file to Lieutenant Fuentes. There's no need for you to go out. . . ."

"Yes there is. My car."

"It can stay where it is until tomorrow."

"I'd rather go get it now."

"You mean right now?"

"Yes."

" . . . All right, if that's what you want."

Emily asked to go along. Kerry put up a mild objection, but this was not a good time for the kid to be alone. We piled into Kerry's car, and she drove us out to Daly City. I thought I might have some kind of flashback reaction when I got to the house again; I felt nothing at all. It was just another tract home wrapped in morning fog, nondescript even with the yellow crime-scene tape strung across the front entrance and a couple of sensation-seekers gawking on the sidewalk nearby.

Kerry pulled up behind my car, and when I opened the passenger door she said, "What now?"

"Go fetch the file for Fuentes, I guess."

"And then?"

"I don't know. I'll see how I feel."

She gnawed at her lower lip. "You won't? . . ."

"Won't what?"

"Nothing. I love you."

"I love you, too. Always."

Emily murmured, "Please come home soon," and I said I would, and they went away. And I was alone.

Instead of going downtown to the agency, I found myself driving aimlessly for a time with the radio tuned to a music station, the volume up high so I would not have to listen to the sounds inside my head. Then, without any conscious intent, I was back in Daly

City—at the police station on Sullivan Avenue. Inside, I asked for Lieutenant Fuentes and was told he was off duty. My name and ID got me an audience with another plainclothesman attached to the Dain case; his name was Erdman. He thought I was there to deliver the file, and when he found out I wasn't and that I had no new information to impart, he adopted that faintly hostile, faintly arrogant attitude some cops have toward citizens they perceive to be uncooperative. He wouldn't tell me anything about the progress of their investigation, despite my personal involvement. Ongoing and privileged, he said. We'll contact you if there are any developments you need to know about, he said. And don't forget to bring that file as soon as possible, he said.

It made me angry. I wanted to say to him, "Listen, you son of a bitch, how would you feel if you'd come within one second of dying last night? You have any idea what it's like to have a revolver misfire when the muzzle's pressed against the back of your head?" But I held my tongue and my temper and walked away from him, out into the thinning fog. He was insensitive, self-involved, but he wasn't my enemy. Right now I had only one person to worry about, and it was not Fuentes or anyone connected with the bald man or even Baldy himself.

The one person, one potential enemy was me.

I sat in the car, reminding myself that I was in a state of crisis, vulnerable and prone to overreaction and misjudgment. I needed to take things very slow, to think carefully before I acted. I needed to maintain perspective and distance. In short, and in spite of what I'd thought and felt in the immediate aftermath last night, I needed to stay out of the investigation and on the sidelines. Let the law handle it—Fuentes, that asshole inside, any other police agency that might come into the case. They'd find Baldy sooner or later. Might have a line on him already. It wasn't my job and I had no real, lasting desire to see him dead or to dance on his grave. Justice, not revenge. Revenge was a fool's game—I'd learned that lesson after my escape from the mountain cabin, at the end of a hunt for the sad, sick bastard responsible for those three months of hell. Since then, I'd grown to hate violence in all its forms, vowed never to harm another living creature. Let a judge and jury pass sentence on Baldy, let society execute him if the sentence was death. Life in prison without possibility of parole would be even more fitting. Years, decades behind bars . . . that was less than he deserved, maybe, but punishment enough for murdering Carolyn Dain and almost murdering me.

Except that he hadn't almost murdered me, he *had* murdered me. The gun misfiring didn't change that. He'd put it to my head, he'd said, "Lay still, you old fuck," meaning lay still forever, you old fuck, and he'd pulled the trigger. Clear intent, cause and effect. I was still alive but he'd murdered me last night.

Then there was Emily. If I'd let her go inside the house with me, or if she'd gotten out of the car too soon and he'd spotted her, he'd have shot her dead, too. A ten-year-old kid, and he'd have executed her without hesitation or compunction. Kill one, kill two— kill three.

Take things slow, think carefully before acting, maintain perspective . . . yes. Stay out of the investigation, let the cops handle it? No. He murdered me, he might have murdered my little girl. How could I stay out of it?

Nobody answered the bell in Annette Byers' apartment. On the mailbox marked 1-A, L. Timmerman, was a Dymo label reading "Bldg Mgr"; I rang that bell. No response there, either. I tried the other apartments, found one woman home, but she hadn't seen Byers yesterday or today, nor anyone answering Jay Cohalan's description.

I drove around the neighborhood, looking for her MG. Gone. Nor was Cohalan's Camry anywhere in evidence. It was possible the two of them were on the run, or maybe holed up someplace together. And just as possible that the Daly City cops had located them, or Cohalan at least had gone in voluntarily when he learned of his wife's death. I had no real reason to suspect the pair anyway, without a definite link between one or both and Baldy.

Saturday-afternoon quiet in the office. I sat at my desk with the paper file on the Dain-Cohalan case spread out in front of me. Tamara kept all our records on computer disk, but in deference to my technophobia, she printed out all pertinent information as well. I kept the printouts for open investigations and those for closed ones dating back six months in my old file cabinet.

Possibilities were what I was looking for—names, details, anything worth checking on. There were two. Annette Byers had not been Cohalan's first extramarital fling, according to what his wife had told me, and my investigation had turned up one other name: Doris Niall, a programmer with a dot-com outfit in his office building. That was before I'd confirmed his relationship with Byers, so I'd had Tamara do a little digging on Ms. Niall. She had a brother who'd been in and out of trouble since he turned sixteen—half a dozen arrests for drug-related offenses, tours in the juvenile detention center and the San Francisco county jail. Steve Niall. Present activities and whereabouts unknown.

The other possibility was a Byers connection. When she'd been busted for selling meth, she hadn't been alone; also arrested in the sting was one Charles Andrew Bright, age 28. She'd got off with little more than probation, but Bright had been slapped with a felony conviction that had gotten him a year as a state minimum-security guest. His relationship with Byers wasn't clear, and I hadn't bothered to clarify it because it hadn't seem relevant at the time.

I looked up both Steve Niall and Bright in the phone directories for San Francisco and half a dozen other Bay Area cities and counties. No listing for either man.

All right. Tamara. I rang the number of the apartment she shared with her cello-playing boyfriend. Nobody home. I left a message to call me as soon as she came in, car phone or home phone. With her computer skills and contacts, it shouldn't take her long, even on the weekend, to track down some of the available data on Niall and Bright. And maybe get a line on what the Daly City cops had turned up so far; she had a friend, Felicia Jackson, who worked in the SFPD's communications department.

And meanwhile?

Deliver the file to the Daly City cops . . . except that after my little run-in with Erdman I had no intention of rushing it out there. I considered other options. Only one had any appeal, the one that called for direct action and held the best chance, slim as it was, for a lead to Baldy.

The bottom drawer of my desk is a catchall for miscellany. I rummaged around in there until I found the pick gun somebody had given me years ago. Eberhardt? I seemed to remember it had come from him when he was still with the SFPD, confiscated from a hot-prowl professional burglar and delivered to me as a birthday joke. Some joke.

A pick gun is a homemade tool that has a hand grip, a trigger, a lockpick for a barrel, and a little knob on top that you twist to adjust the spring tension. Insert the lockpick and pull the trigger, and the pick moves up and down at a rapid speed; when you have the tension just right, it bounces all the pins in a cylinder lock at once. It's a lot faster than using hand picks and tension bars to release the pins one at a time, but less reliable. It doesn't work in all locks, deadbolts and most newer varieties, and like Baldy's revolver last night it has a tendency to jam. Most professional burglars refuse to use one. I had never used this one or any other myself; I'd kept Eberhardt's little present as a souvenir, not a functional business tool. I'm not the kind of detective who believes in illegal trespass, except in extreme circumstances.

Like mine, now.

When you're hunting your own murderer, anything goes.

8

ON THE WAY OUT CALIFORNIA I STOPPED AT A neighborhood hardware store and bought a can of 3-in-1 oil. The pick gun had gone unused for so long it needed lubrication. I helped myself to one of the free shopping papers from a rack at the storefront, spread it open on the car seat. A couple of shots of oil, then I tested the trigger action, pick movement, and tension knob. Still a little balky. I gave it another squirt, wiped off the excess, tried it again. Seemed to work okay then, but whether or not it would get me into Annette Byers' building and her apartment was still problematical.

I was on Locust Street, scouting for a parking place, when the car phone buzzed. Tamara. I made myself listen patiently to her expressions of concern, delivered the appropriate responses, then told her what I wanted her to do.

She said, "How come you don't trust the cops to find this bald guy?"

"It's not that I don't trust them. They've got their resources, we've got ours—we might be able to turn up a lead before they do. Besides, I shouldn't've held on to that damn money in the first place, no matter what the client wanted. I feel responsible."

"For the woman's death? Might've happened anyway."

"And it might not have."

"Not your fault."

"I know that, but I still feel responsible."

Three-beat. Then, "You sound like a man with an agenda."

"Meaning what? That this is personal? Damn right it is."

"What happens if you find him before the law does?"

"Nothing happens. I'm not a vigilante, Tamara."

"I know it, but do the cops? Does the bald dude?"

"You going to give me an argument?"

"No sir, not me." In a softer voice she said, "Must've been pretty bad last night."

"Yeah, pretty bad. Can you get to work right away?"

"Nothing on my plate except what's left of a crappy pizza. I'll see if I can get hold of Felicia first thing."

"Call me as soon as you find out anything. If I don't answer, keep trying until I do."

I was on Clay now, a couple of blocks from Byers' building, and I spotted a parking space opposite the Presidio Heights Playground—the first I'd come across in ten minutes of circling. Tight fit, but I got the car maneuvered into it. The fog had all but burned off here; I walked to Locust through pale sunshine and blustery wind, the pick gun in one pocket and my .38 in the other.

Still nobody home. Or at least nobody answering the bell. The vestibule, the sidewalk, the street in front—all empty. I stooped to peer at the locking mechanism on the entrance doors. Flush-mounted cylinder lock, a steel lip on the doorframe to protect the bolt and striking plate. It had been there awhile, seen a lot of use; that was good because pick guns work best in old locks.

I unpocketed the thing, slid the pick into the keyhole, worked the knob to adjust the tension, and squeezed the trigger. It made a small chattering noise, vibrating in my hand, but nothing happened. I fiddled with the knob, tried again. Nothing. Another adjustment, another squeeze. Nothing. I gritted my teeth, got set to try again. And stopped and just stood there.

For Christ's sake, I thought, what am I doing?

The angle of daylight was such that the door glass acted as a mirror: my cloudy reflection stared back at me. I was sweating and I looked a little wild-eyed and the facial Band-Aids and bruises completed an image to frighten children. Standing here with a burglar tool in my hand like a demented sneak thief, hearing clicks in my head instead of voices.

"You damn fool," I said under my breath, but that only added to the Halloween image. Not thinking clearly. Not acting like a rational man or a professional detective. Get a grip, goddamn it!

I put the pick gun away in my pocket, cleaned the sweat off my face. All right, use your brain. Think. There are other ways to get into a building, into a locked apartment. Risky, all of them, but a hell of a lot more reasonable than playing stupid Watergate games in broad daylight.

I took a couple of slow breaths, calming down, and then rang the bell for 1-A, L. Timmerman, Bldg Mgr. And this time a male voice said through the intercom, "Yes?"

"Mr. Timmerman?"

"Yes, what is it?"

"Police business."

There was a murmur that might have been "Oh, shit." After which he said, "Right away," and the door buzzer sounded.

Just like that, you horse's ass, you.

I went in, and a skinny guy about fifty with protuberant front teeth like a beaver's was coming out of a door labeled 1-A. Before he shut the door I could hear noise from a TV set tuned to a college football game, crowd sounds and the overheated voices of a pair of announcers. When he got a good look at me he blinked and his jaw dropped an inch or so. He said in a surprisingly deep baritone, "What happened to you?"

I told him the truth. "Run-in with a dangerous felon."

"I hope he got the worst of it."

"Not yet, but he will."

"You here about the Byers woman?"

"That's right."

"Well, I told that lieutenant, what's his name, Fumente. . . ."

"Fuentes."

"Right, Fuentes. I told him and the city cop . . . uh, officer with him everything I know early this morning. Which isn't much. Like I said to them, I mind my own business."

"I'd like a look inside her apartment, Mr. Timmerman. Check on something that might have been overlooked. You mind opening it up for me?"

Ticklish moment. If he asked to see ID, I'd show him my investigator's license with my thumb over the part that said I was a private not public detective. If he wanted to see the entire license or a badge, I would back off and walk away. Impersonating a police officer is a felony; so far I hadn't made that claim, at least not directly, and I wouldn't if push came to shove.

But he'd already taken me at face value. And he was anxious to cooperate; he didn't want trouble with the law any more than I did. He said, "No, sir, I don't mind. Just let me get my passkey."

On the second floor, when he'd finished unlocking the door to Byers' studio, I said, "You go on about your business, Mr. Timmerman. I'll let you know when I'm done so you can lock up again."

"Sure thing. Take your time. I'm not going anywhere today, just watching the Cal game on TV."

The apartment seemed even more disarrayed than it had on Thursday night, but probably not as a result of the police visit. The Chinese partition had been knocked askew, revealing the bed—a double without a headboard—and the fact that the none-too-clean sheets and blankets had been pulled loose and were trailing on the floor, either by a restless sleeper or as the result of vigorous love-making. In the wall behind the bed a closet door stood open; most of the hangers in there appeared to be empty. Next to the closet was a cheap maple dresser, all its drawers open, part of a black net brassiere caught on the knob of one.

I moved over there for a closer look. All that remained in the closet were a couple of inexpensive dresses, a blouse that lay crumpled on the floor, and a pair of scuffed sandals. Three of the dresser drawers had been cleaned out; the fourth contained the black bra, some wadded-up pantyhose, and the husks of two long-dead flies.

Packed up and long gone, I thought. In a hurry, from the looks of it.

In the bathroom I opened the medicine cabinet. The usual clutter, but no toothbrush or prescription medicines or other essentials. Nothing essential to me, either. I wasted a couple of minutes checking inside the toilet tank and other possible hiding places, doing it out of thoroughness rather than hope. If there'd been anything to find, Fuentes and the San Francisco cop would have turned it up this morning.

I went out to the kitchenette. The lid to the tape compartment on the answering machine was open; if Byers had replaced the tape I'd confiscated on Thursday, Fuentes had carted the new one away. I poked through drawers and then took them all the way out to see if anything had been taped underneath or behind. Looked inside the cupboards, the small refrigerator, and the even smaller stove. Peered into corners and crannies. Nothing. Under the sink was a garbage bag about a third full. The contents didn't appear to have been disturbed; the two cops had either overlooked or ignored the bag. I used two fingers on each hand to sift through it.

Coffee grounds, empty cans, a shriveled apple, a sour-smelling half-and-half container, a few wadded-up yellow sheets from the five-by-seven pad by the phone. And another sheet from the pad that had been folded and torn into several little pieces. The wadded ones were meaningless—part of a grocery list, tic-tac-toe games, and the kind of doodles people make when they're talking on the phone. I fished out as many of the torn scraps as I could find and fitted them together, puzzle fashion, on the breakfast bar until I could read what was written there.

Dingo 4.15 V.V.S.

Meaningless, too, maybe. And maybe not. The 4.15 could be a time . . . a reminder to meet somebody named Dingo at V.V.S., whatever that was. Or was it some kind of code message? The hand-writing was Byers'—same as the grocery list—and the fact that it had been torn up rather than wadded like the other throwaways made me wonder if she'd done it to make sure somebody— Cohalan?—didn't happen to see it. I scraped the pieces together, slipped them into my wallet.

There was nothing else for me here. After I put the garbage bag back where I'd found it, I made one more pass through the studio just to make sure and then got out of there.

Downstairs I knocked on Timmerman's door. He said when he opened up, "All through?" He didn't seem particularly interested; he had one ear cocked to the football game blaring away behind him, the crowd and the announcers engaging in the kind of frenzy that follows a touchdown.

"All through. You can lock up any time."

"Yes, sir. Right away."

On my way to the car I wondered if he would mention me if the police contacted him again. If he did, they could make trouble for me with the State Board of Licenses. Worry about that if and when. Right now it didn't seem to matter much.

I was halfway to Daly City when Tamara called again. She said, "I tried you a little while ago. Not much yet, but a couple of things you be wanting to know."

"Go ahead."

"Felicia's working today and I got her to access the DCPD computer for us. Data's incomplete, but as of two P.M. they still didn't have an ID on your perp, and Cohalan and Byers hadn't come forward or been located. Lieutenant Fuentes put out a BOLO on both of 'em."

BOLO is police code for a Be on Lookout order. "When?" I asked.

"Around noon."

"County wide, Bay Area, statewide?"

"Bay Area so far."

Byers and Cohalan, I thought. On the run together? Unlawful flight to avoid answering for . . . what? The extortion scam? Involvement in the money theft and Carolyn Dain's murder? They'd run if they were accessories to a capital crime; they might also run if they were innocent and afraid they'd be tabbed for it. In any case, a noon BOLO was next to worthless. With an early-morning jump, they could be in Nevada or L.A. or closing in on the Oregon border by now.

"Anything on Byers?" I asked.

"Not much more than what we had before. Born in Lodi, raised there by an alcoholic single mother. Father unknown. Mother died when she was in high school, no other known relatives. First arrest at nineteen, possession of marijuana. Meth bust was her only felony charge."

"Niall and Bright?"

"Sketchy stuff so far."

"Keep digging. Addresses, first priority."

"One other thing," she said. "I accessed the office machine to check for messages. Man named Melvin Bishop called, said he's a friend of Carolyn Dain and wants to talk to you."

Melvin. Mel. Last night's anxious caller, probably. "He say what about?"

"No. Sounded real shook up."

"Leave an address or just a phone number?"

"Both. Address is 750 De Montfort. I looked it up—it's off Ocean out near City College. Said he'd be there all weekend."

"Okay. Here's something else for you to look into. See if you can find a link between Byers and somebody or something called Dingo."

"Dingo? Like the Australian wild dog?"

"D-i-n-g-o."

"That's how they spell it Down Under. Kind of appropriate if it's somebody's name, huh? Bitch like Annette Byers hanging with a wild dog?"

At the DCPD I left the file with the desk sergeant and beat it out of there as though I was nothing more than a messenger boy. I did not want another session with Fuentes or Erdman or any other cop today, not after my previous visit and not in my frame of mind.

The car phone buzzed as I pulled out of the parking lot. Kerry, this time. "I just wanted to hear your voice," she said. "You okay?"

"Holding up."

"Where are you?"

"Driving around at the moment. I went to the office, did a little work."

"When're you coming home?"

"Not for a while. Maybe not until tomorrow. I thought I might spend the night at my flat."

There was a longish pause before she said, "You think that's a good idea? Being alone tonight?"

"I'm not sure yet. I'll have to see how I feel later."

"Call before seven and let me know. So we won't wait dinner if you're not coming."

"I will."

I felt better for having heard her voice. God, I loved that woman. She was the rock-solid center of my life, whether we were together or not. Without her I would be in worse shape right now than I was.

In my head I heard the clicks again.

Yeah. Much worse shape.

9

DE MONTFORT WAS A SHORT RESIDENTIAL street of older, lower middle-class homes. Most were two-story wooden affairs with long staircases in front, but number 750 turned out to be a squatty one-story stucco in the pseudo-Spanish style of the thirties. It looked out of place in the neighborhood. So did the man who opened the door to my ring. He was slender, fair-haired, handsome in a sad-eyed, ascetic way. Black-rimmed glasses pushed low over the bridge of an aquiline nose gave him a professorial air. His face was smooth and unlined; he might have been anywhere from thirty-five to forty-five.

"It's good of you to come by," he said when I identified myself. Then he said, squinting at me through his glasses, "My God, that bastard did a job on you, didn't he."

More of a job than you'll ever know. But all I said was, "Yes."

"Come in, come in."

The interior smelled of flowers, or maybe flower-scented air freshener. The patterned wallpaper in the hallway and in the living room he led me into looked at least fifty years old. Most of the furniture was of the same vintage, but well-preserved. The room was neat, clean; an arrangement of purple and yellow flowers sat atop one of the tables. Family photographs and others depicting antiquated street and cable cars and municipal railway buses adorned two of the walls.

"This was my parents' home," Bishop said. "I inherited it when my mother died. My dad worked for Muni for forty years." He made a vague gesture with one hand. "I really should redecorate. Either that, or sell the place and move into something smaller. But I can't seem to bring myself to do either one. Changing or leaving the home where you grew up is never easy."

"I suppose not."

"Sit down, please. Anywhere you like. Something to drink? Coffee, tea, pop? I have beer or wine. . . ."

"Nothing, thanks."

I lowered myself into an armchair. Bishop waited until I was settled before occupying a high-backed sofa. He crossed his legs, sighed, shook his head. "I can't believe Carolyn's gone," he said. "Shot that way, in her own home . . . Christ."

"The two of you were close, I take it."

"Yes, we were. Very close."

"I figured as much since she spent Thursday night with you."

" . . . How did you know that? Did she tell you?"

"No. Educated guess. I was there when you called last night. How long have you been seeing her?"

"Seeing her?"

"Having the affair with her."

His eyes, a watery blue, blinked at me in a startled way. "Affair? Good Lord, is that what you think?" He drew himself up and said, "You couldn't be more wrong. As a matter of fact, I'm gay."

I should have seen it coming; the signs were obvious enough. But my powers of observation, like my thinking, were subpar today. I said, "Oh," because that was the only thing that came into my head.

"Why do you say it like that? Does it bother you?"

"No. Why should it?"

"Well, your expression and your tone. . . ."

"Took me by surprise, that's all."

He peered at me for a few seconds; then his body slumped again. "I didn't mean to snap at you," he said. "I'm not usually one who sees homophobia everywhere he looks." He repeated the vague gesture. "I guess I'm overly sensitive and defensive today. Angry and feeling vulnerable."

"I feel the same way."

"Yes, of course you do. In my case . . . I'm just so sick and tired of losing people I care about. My parents, two friends to AIDS, Roger, and now Carolyn."

"Roger?"

"A man with whom I had a long-term relationship." He said it matter-of-factly, but the words were underscored with bitterness. "He's not really dead, but he might as well be as far as I'm concerned."

There was nothing for me to say to that.

"Lost love, shattered dreams," Bishop said. It sounded self-pitying, but I had the feeling it wasn't. "Carolyn understood. All too well. That's one of the bonds we had. More than once we cried on each other's shoulders."

"How did the two of you meet?"

"White Rock School. I'm also an instructor there—history, social studies, political science."

"And she confided in you about her marriage?"

"Oh, yes. She had no one else to talk to, you see. No close friends, no living relatives. That was another bond we shared. Lonely people naturally gravitate to each other, particularly those in the same line of work."

"About her marriage, Mr. Bishop."

"Well, it was difficult for her. Very difficult. I told her she would be much better off if she left Jay, but she couldn't bring herself to do it. She believed in seeing a commitment through, no matter how unpleasant it became. I understood that. I doubt I could have left Roger if he hadn't walked out. Love makes fools of us all."

"Sometimes."

"Not always, that's true. We were just two of the unlucky ones. But my God, I never thought he'd do anything to cause her to die."

"He may not be the one who caused her death, except indirectly."

"That crazy scheme of his to take away her inheritance . . . I warned her that's what it was, a scheme, but she needed to give him the benefit of the doubt. Until it became too obvious for her to ignore and she went to see you. But even then. . . ."

"There's no evidence yet to prove that Cohalan was involved in what happened last night."

Bishop frowned. "You mean you don't believe he was?"

"I didn't say that. Just that there's no evidence yet."

"But who else, if not Jay?"

"I don't know. I was hoping that was why you wanted to see me— that you have some information that might help me find out who's responsible."

"No. I wish I did, but . . . no."

"Then why did you ask to see me?"

"I thought *you* could tell *me* something." The vague gesture again; it was obviously habitual with him. "I needed to talk to someone and you . . . I thought . . . I'm sorry if I misled you."

"Don't apologize, Mr. Bishop. I understand."

"Do you?"

I nodded. He was a bleeder, too. Not the Cohalan and Byers leech variety—the sensitive, empathetic type like me who leaks soul blood when deeply wounded. The difference between us was that his reaction was passive, his anger impotent; he had to reach out to others to help staunch the flow and cauterize the wound. I had to do the job directly, with minimal aid from others. Bleeder, heal thyself.

"Do you know if Carolyn told anyone besides you about the cash?" I asked him. "That I had it and was going to deliver it to her yesterday?"

"No, I'm sure she didn't. She came straight here after she spoke to you Thursday night."

"She didn't call anyone, talk to anyone?"

"Just me. We sat up most of the night talking."

"And you're sure you didn't let it slip to anybody?"

"Oh, God, no. I'd never betray a confidence like that, not even accidentally. I'm too cautious for that."

I said, "I understand Cohalan was chronically unfaithful."

"Chronically is the right word."

"Did she know any of the women?"

"I doubt it. She never mentioned any specific person."

"I have to ask this. Did she ever retaliate in kind?"

"Take a lover of her own? Not Carolyn. She was the most moral person I've ever known." He added sadly, "And the most forgiving."

"Did you know Cohalan uses methamphetamines?"

"She told me, yes," Bishop said. "Another chronic fault. I swear, she was a saint to have put up with that man."

"Would you have any idea who supplied him?"

"With drugs? No."

"Would Carolyn have revealed a name if she'd known?"

"She might have. Yes."

"Charles Bright. That name ring any bells?"

He thought about it before shaking his head.

"Steve Niall?"

Same consideration, same negative.

"How about Dingo?"

"I don't . . . Dingo?"

"Like the Australian wild dog."

"No. I'm sure I've never heard that name from Carolyn or anyone else. All these people . . . who are they?"

I said, "Possible drug connections," and let it go at that. "Anything else you can tell me? Anything at all she might have confided about her husband, his affairs, his drug use?"

He didn't answer immediately; his expression said he was

working his memory. And he pinched something out of it that brought a sudden glint to his eyes. "There is one thing. I don't know if it's important, but. . . ." He got abruptly to his feet. "Wait here, I'll be right back."

I stayed in the armchair for about a minute before restlessness drove me out of it. I paced around, looking at the framed photographs without really seeing what was in them. On my third circuit, Bishop reappeared and came quickly to where I was.

"Carolyn found this about three weeks ago," he said, holding out a small, round object. "In a pair of Jay's trousers. She thought I might know what it is and brought it to school and forgot it when she left my office. I meant to return it, but she didn't ask for it, and I forgot it, too, until just now."

The object was brown, made of smooth, shiny plastic, about the size of a poker chip. On one side, in black, were the words *Lucky Buffalo Chip*. On the other side, a red line drawing of a grinning horned bull wearing a ten-gallon cowboy hat; underneath, in a half circle along the edge, more black printing: *Remember the Alamo!*

Bishop asked hopefully, "Does it mean anything to you?"

"No."

"Nor to me. It reminds me of those tokens they give out in Nevada casinos, good for free plays on the blackjack and roulette tables. But gambling isn't one of Jay's vices—the only one he doesn't have, I'm sure."

"Doesn't look like a casino token," I said, "despite the 'lucky.' Some kind of advertising gimmick, maybe."

"I can't imagine what for."

Neither could I at the moment. I said, "Do you mind if I keep this?"

"By all means, if you think it might help."

I tucked it into my wallet with the note scraps from Byers' studio. Bishop showed me to the door and then said, "May I ask you something?"

"Go ahead."

"When you find the man who killed Carolyn and hurt you . . . will you be all right?"

I didn't have to ask him what he meant. He was a perceptive man; he had me pegged, too. "For that part of it, yes."

"And afterward?"

"I think so."

"A survivor," he said.

"I have been so far."

"As have I. So far."

We shook hands solemnly, like brothers saying good-bye.

Tamara said, "Where you at? Sounds noisy."

It was noisy. I was in a busy service station on Ocean Avenue, feeding another load of black gold into the gas tank. Two trucks and an M line street car were rumbling by just then. And at the pumps ahead of me, a woman was loudly complaining to her passenger about the outrageous gas prices, saying that what they amounted to was consumer rape. She'd get no argument from me.

"Just a second," I said to Tamara, and rolled up the window. "Okay, better. What have you got?"

"Current address for Steve Niall. Seven-twelve Natoma. The Southwick Hotel."

"Skid Row."

"Crime doesn't pay, huh?"

"Neither does stupidity, in the long run. You call the Southwick to make sure he's still living there?"

"My mama didn't raise no incompetent babies," she said. "I called, he's registered. Clerk doesn't seem to like the man much. Sneered all over himself when I asked."

"Anything on Charles Bright?"

"Goes by Charlie, first of all. Paroled last March. No hit on his current whereabouts. I did get the name of his parole officer, but civil servants don't work weekends, right? Want me to try to get hold of the PO at home?"

"Not much point. He wouldn't give out any information over the phone. What's the name?"

"Ben Duryea."

"Good, I know Ben. I'll look him up if necessary."

"Still checking Bright's personal life and drug BG," she said. "Born in Texas, home of Dubya and those other Cowboys. Broken home, father died of a heroin overdose. Genetic disposition to controlled substances, you know what I'm saying? Moved out here when he was sixteen, got his ass in trouble right away, been there ever since."

"History of violence?"

"None on his record. User and small-time dealer, strictly—meth, blow, whatever. Walking pharmaceutical company."

"What's his relationship with Annette Byers?"

"Only connection I can find so far is they were both busted on the meth sting."

I signed off and went to pay the gas tariff. Thirty-two bucks for fifteen gallons. If the prices kept climbing, as was being predicted, there were going to be riots one day. You could get away with disarming Californians, and taking away social services and most vices, and raising taxes to the limit, and jacking up gas and electric bills 10 percent or more, but the one thing they wouldn't stand for was pricing them out of their cars.

10

SKID ROW WAS A BAD PLACE FOR ME TODAY. On my best days its filthy sidewalks and gallery of bleak, wasted lives creates a dark and depressive mood in me. And this was anything but one of my best days.

A few years ago I'd come down here to see a small-time bleeder, ex-con, and self-proclaimed religious convert named Eddie Quinlan. One of the shadow men without substance or purpose who drift along the narrow catwalk that separates conventional society from the underworld. When he'd asked to see me, I thought it was because he had something he wanted to sell; I'd bought information from him from time to time for a few dollars a pop, in the days before Tamara and the Internet. But that wasn't what he wanted that time. He bent my ear for half an hour about the things and the people he saw every day from the window of his Sixth Street hotel room—the crack and smack deals, the drunk-rolling and mugging, the petty thievery, the acts of sexual degradation. "Souls burning everywhere you go," was the way he'd described the hookers, pimps, addicts, dealers, drunks, and worse. Doomed souls who were dooming others to burn with them.

Quinlan's comments that night had seemed rambling and pointless, and I'd left him without a clear idea of why he'd asked to see me. I found out a few hours later. Among the last things he'd said to me was, "You want to do something, you know? You want to try to fix it somehow, put out the fires. There has to be a way." He'd found a way, all right. He'd used a high-powered semiautomatic rifle to shoot down fourteen men and women from his window. Nine dead on the scene, one dead later in the hospital—all with criminal records. And Eddie Quinlan had made himself the last victim, another burning soul, with a bullet through his own brain.

I've hated coming to Skid Row ever since. There was nothing I could have done to stop Quinlan, even if I'd had a clue to what was on his mind. Yet I was part of it just the same. He'd called me because he wanted somebody to help him justify what he was about to do; somebody to record a kind of verbal suicide note and who could be trusted to pass it on afterward, to the police and the media. And of course that was just what I'd done.

This little corner of urban hell was not as bad as it had been back then. The cops, the politicians, and the real-estate boom and tech-nomoney that had reclaimed much of the South of Market area had all had a hand in cleaning up and shrinking Skid Row to some extent. Now there was not quite so much street crime and wide-open drug dealing. But the addicts and pushers were still here, in alleyways and behind closed doors; so were the drunks leaning against walls in tight little clusters, the muttering mental cases, and all the others who had no place to go, no hope, only the bare exposed threads of humanity left. Many of the cheap hotels and greasy spoons and seedy taverns and barred-window liquor stores and porn theaters were still here, too. So was the effluvium of despair, the faint brimstone stink of souls burning.

Natoma is an alley that runs parallel between Mission and Howard for several blocks, through the heart of Skid Row. The Southwick Hotel was between Sixth and Seventh, a four-story residence hotel not quite as old or scabrous as the Majestic where

Eddie Quinlan had lived and murdered and died. The lobby was similar—small, the only furniture a couple of crusty upholstered chairs that looked as though no one ever sat in them except spiders and roaches. The usual swamp-gas stench of disinfectant closed my throat as I crossed to a counter with an ancient rack of cubbyhole slots and a closed door behind it.

There was no sign of anybody until I slammed my palm down on a corroded bell. Then the door opened, and a guy about my age appeared in slow, wary movements. He had a smooth, round, unlined, benign face fringed with curly white hair—and the eyes of a maniac in a slasher movie. The contrast was both startling and disturbing, as if a war were going on inside him, his own private Armageddon, and the forces of evil were winning.

He didn't say anything, just stood there looking at me out of those iniquitous eyes. I don't flinch or look away from any man, but it was a small effort to keep my gaze locked with his as I said, "Steve Niall."

"Not here," in a voice as crusty as the two chairs.

"Where can I find him?"

Instead of answering he put his back to me and pretended to check the contents of the cubbyhole slots.

I said, tight and hard, "Turn around and look at me, Pop. Take a good, close look."

For a few beats he didn't move. Then, in that slow, wary way of his, he did what I'd told him to. The evil eyes crawled over me. His mouth quirked slightly, not quite a sneer, and he said, "Cop?"

"Close enough. Where can I find Steve Niall?"

"What you want with him? He do something?"

"Answer my question."

"He's an asshole. You gonna bust him?"

"Answer the goddamn question."

He hesitated, but he did not want trouble with the law. Or with me, the way I looked. He said, "Rick's Tattoo Parlor. Fifth and Folsom."

"Niall work there?"

"Hangs out there. He don't *work* anywhere."

"Where else does he hang out, just in case?"

The clerk shrugged. "He's around, like a bad smell. You'll find him."

"If I don't, I'll be back."

He shrugged again; his mouth said, "I ain't going nowhere," and his eyes told me to go screw myself. I told him the same thing with mine. That's the thing about evil, even this mild, diluted variety: face it head on, and a little of it gets into you as if by osmosis. Face the pure kind too often, and if you're not careful, it can start Armageddon inside you, too.

The section along Folsom, stretching south and east from Fifth, has been in a state of flux for several years. Not so long ago it was a semi-industrial, semi-residential part of Skid Row; then the rough-trade S&M and gay nightclub scene moved in; now it was starting to resemble nearby South Beach, the South of Market area, and Mission Bay, showing evidence of the tentacle-like encroachment of technology-related firms, buildings converted into combination office-and-living space, and wannabe trendy restaurants and clubs. Of all the rapid-growth changes in the city these days, the gentrifi-cation of this area, what oldtimers call South of the Slot, was prob-ably the most desirable.

Rick's Tattoo Parlor was a leftover from the old days, a hole-in-the-wall squeezed between a couple of other leftovers—a Chinese takeout joint and a cheap liquor store masquerading as a neighbor-hood grocery. Red and blue lettering in the single window adver-tised "Rick's Specialties": Body Piercing, Full Body Portraits, and something called Body Frosting.

The interior was a long single room, brightly lit; a closed door in the back wall said there was another room or office behind it. The walls were covered with framed designs, hundreds of them in color and black and white. There were two big chairs, a cross between armchairs and barber chairs; in one of them a guy with yellow spiked hair, dressed in a leather vest over a bare torso and a pair of black leather pants, was having his left biceps tattooed with what looked like the gay pride symbol in a chain-bordered square. The man manipulating the electric needle, a complicated arrangement that fit over his hand like a set of brass knuckles, was in his late twenties, had greasy black hair pulled back into a ponytail, and was a walking advertisement for his art. He wore an armless T-shirt that displayed arms, shoulders, and neck bristling with gaudy tattoos. His entire left arm and shoulder was a fire-breathing dragon in green and red and bright orange; something that resembled a Rubens nude reclining on a bed of lettuce writhed and wriggled on his right forearm.

The needle made a humming, buzzing noise. Over it, without looking at me, he said, "With you in a minute. Almost done here."

"Are you Rick?"

"Yeah. Just hang on, man."

"I'm looking for Steve Niall."

"Steve?" He glanced at me then, but I was nobody he knew; he returned his attention to his artwork. "Not here."

"Where can I find him?"

"Man, I can't talk and work. Hang on, okay?"

Okay. I hung on by looking at some of the framed designs. Labels identified one batch as Polynesian Tribal, another as Pure Fantasy, another as Traditional Seafarer. There were animals and cars and weapons and circus performers and film stars and a slew of X-rated items. Why anybody would want to walk around with an image of a copulating couple emblazoned on his skin was beyond me. Rick still hadn't finished with the yellow-haired customer, and I was losing patience; but pushing him while he was creating on his human canvas would only buy me hostility. I picked up a magazine from a stack on a table, a trade publication called *Skin & Ink,* and leafed through it until the humming and buzzing finally quit.

Yellow-hair liked the finished tattoo and said so; money changed hands and he went out, making a kissy mouth at me on the way.

Cute. The world is full of smart-ass jerks of all genders, ages, and sexual orientation.

Rick had the same wary look as the Southwick's desk clerk, but without the evil eyes; his expression said he couldn't quite figure me out. Point in my favor. "So you're looking for Steve," he said.

"That's right."

"How come?"

"I've got business with him."

"What kind of business?"

"What kind do you think?"

"You tell me, man."

"Steve's business. My business."

"Might be mine, too," he said.

"I don't think so." I was feeling my way along, but I thought the handling was right. "Look, Rick, I can pay for what I want. If you've got a cut coming, get it from Steve."

"Not you, huh?"

"Not me. Tell me where I can find him or I go to somebody else."

"He know you?"

A lie on that was too easy to get tripped up on. I said, "No. We've got a mutual acquaintence."

"Yeah? Who's that?"

"Jay Cohalan."

"Who?"

"Cohalan. Jay Cohalan."

"Name don't ring any bells."

"He used to sleep with Steve's sister."

"Yeah? Uh, Candy?"

"No, Doris. Steve's sister Doris."

He relaxed. Flexed both shoulders and his right arm in a way that caused the Rubens nude to wriggle suggestively. It wasn't a bed of lettuce she was reclining on, I noticed then. It was a bower of broad, thick leaves like those of a banana plant.

"Okay," he said, "so you're in the market."

"I'm in the market."

"What's your pleasure, man?"

"That's for me to tell Steve."

"Yeah," he said. He did that flexing trick again and then slid his gaze over a clock above the rear door. "Almost four. You know O'Key's?"

"No."

"Bar on Eleventh off Howard. Steve should be there by now. One of the booths." I nodded, and he added, "Tell him I sent you. That way I get mine."

"Yeah," I said.

Rick made the nude wriggle one last time before I went out. And wink, by God, something I wouldn't have thought possible. A god-damn come-hither wink.

O'Key's was one of a dying breed, the kind of dark, dingy, brass-railed, creosote-floored watering hole that had once flourished South of the Slot. With its high ceiling and long, mirrored backbar and tall wooden booths, it reminded me of the old city newspaper saloons—Breen's, Hanno's, Jerry & Johnny, and the last of them, the M&M Tavern, that had finally gone under last year. But O'Key's had never been anything more than a workingman's neighborhood bar, that through neglect and attrition had degenerated into just another downscale saloon peopled with individuals to whom drinking was no longer a social pleasure but a way of life and death.

A dozen or so men and women were bellied up to the bar, but none of them was big, bald, hairy-browed. And none paid any attention to me; they had eyes only for the liquid escape in front of them. Two of the booths were occupied, a dispirited-looking couple in one and a lone man in the other. The loner was young and thin and rabbity, with a spade-sharp chin adorned by a scraggly goatee.

I'd gone in there tensed, wary, ready for anything; I let the edge come off a little as I elbowed space at the bar. I bought a beer from the fat bartender, carried it over to the loner's booth.

He was smoking a cigarette in quick, almost furtive drags. It's illegal now to smoke in bars and other public places in this state, but the patrons of joints like O'Key's would flaunt laws a lot more enforceable than that one. Up close, he had a kind of oily sheen that changed my impression of him from rabbity to ratty. He was an odd mix of truncated and elongated: short, small, with delicate hands, tiny ears, a mouth like a hole poked in clay by somebody's thumb; long arms, that sharp chin, a long, narrow nose. A single black hair grew at a bent angle from one nostril like a miniature periscope. I didn't care to speculate on what might be living up there trying to peer out.

When he realized he had company his head jerked up, and he stared at me. I said, "Steve Niall?"

"Who wants to know?"

I sat down across from him without answering. He didn't like that; it made him even more nervous. "Hey," he said, "I'm expectin' somebody, man."

"I'm here now."

"Who're you? What the hell you want?"

"Rick told me I could find you here."

"Yeah? Rick who?"

"I'm in no mood for games, Stevie."

He started to slide out of the booth. I leaned toward him, putting my hands flat on the scarred tabletop. What he saw in my face decided him to stay put; he blinked several times, as if I were an apparition he was trying to make disappear. He was afraid of me, but it was nothing personal. He'd always be afraid of anyone bigger and stronger, any sort of authority figure.

He said again, with a whiny note in his voice, "What the hell you want?"

"The answers to some questions. Then I'll leave you alone to make your deals."

"I dunno what you're talkin' about, deals."

"Grass, crank, speed, whatever your specialty is."

He jerked his gaze around, but nobody else was listening.

"Jesus," he said, "keep your voice down. I dunno what you're talkin' about, I told you."

I swallowed a mouthful of beer. Out of the bottle; I wouldn't have used the glass that had come with it unless it had been sterilized first. "First question," I said. "Guy about forty, big, bald, bushy eyebrows, breath that says he likes onions. Know him?"

"No."

"Don't lie to me, Stevie. No lies, no bullshit."

"I ain't lying, man. I don't know nobody looks like that."

I was watching him closely. The nervous frown appeared genuine; the denial sounded genuine. "All right. Second question: How long since you've seen Jay Cohalan?"

"Who's Jay Cohalan?"

"What'd I just say about lies and bullshit? We both know Cohalan used to date your sister Doris."

" . . . Oh, yeah. Him."

"How long since you've seen him?"

"Long time. Year and a half, maybe. Good fuckin' riddance."

"Why good riddance?"

"You gonna make trouble for him, I hope?"

"Maybe. Why do you care?"

"He jammed up my sister, that's why."

"Jammed her up how?"

"Never told her he was married for one thing," Niall said. "Hit her hard when she found out. She was in love with the bastard, Christ knows why."

"What else?"

He leaned forward and lowered his voice to a near whisper. "He got her hooked on crystal meth. That's nasty shit, man. Took her a while to get straight again."

"He get it from you?"

"Me?" Niall's mouth twitched; it made the long nose hair dance obscenely. "You think I'd supply shit like that to a guy going around with my own sister?"

"Where'd he get it then. Charlie Bright?"

"Who?"

"You heard me. Charlie Bright."

"I don't know nobody named Bright."

Straight answer, I thought. "How about Annette Byers?"

"Her, neither."

"She's Cohalan's new girlfriend. Jammed up on crank, too."

"Yeah? His doing?"

"That's right," I lied.

"Yeah, well, that asshole come sucking around me after Doris dumped him, wanted me to sell him some crank. You believe it? After what he done to her?"

"What'd you tell him?"

"Fuck off, that's what I told him. He knew I don't mess with that shit. No crank, no crack, I ain't that stupid. But he wouldn't go away. Offered me fifty for a name, a connection. So I fixed him up. Yeah, I fixed him good."

"How?"

"Sent his ass to Jackie Spoons. You know Jackie Spoons?"

"Enforcer for Nick Kinsella, isn't he?"

"Used to be, but he branched out three, four years ago. Rough trade, Jackie Spoons. Hooked in with some real bad guys."

"And you sent Cohalan to him."

"Give him Jackie's name. What happened after that, I don't know. I hope he got jammed up like he jammed up Doris."

"Where can I find Jackie Spoons?"

"Can't tell you that. He moves around, you know?"

"Point me to somebody who might know."

"I can't, man. Guys like Jackie, they're outta my league. I'm strictly lightweight. You play in that league, you can end up dead real easy."

"Okay. One more name and I'm gone. Dingo."

"Never heard it."

"Think a little. Dingo."

He thought and said again, "Never heard it."

I took another swallow of beer and then slid out of the booth. Niall looked relieved, but that didn't stop him from opening his mouth.

"Listen," he said, "what's this all about? Who are you, anyway?"

"You really want to know?"

His eyes flicked over my face, flicked away again in a hurry. "Maybe not."

"Definitely not. You don't want to play in my league, either."

I left him lighting another coffin nail with twitchy fingers. Small man, small mind, lightweight in every respect. The kind destined for failure in any league he played in, even the low minors where he was playing now.

11

IN THE CAR, DRIVING AGAIN.

Jackie Spoons. I'd seen him twice, briefly; exchanged maybe half a dozen words with him the second time. But I remembered him well enough. He was not a man you were likely to forget. Big, very big: four or five inches over six feet, weight around 250 and not much of it fat. Ex-heavyweight pug, determined iron pumper. More than just hard-ass muscle, though, or so the rumor had it. Shrewd and ruthless, a deadly combination in his rough-trade world. It didn't surprise me that he'd branched out into drug dealing or that he'd picked the crystal meth crowd to join. They were the hardest of the hardcases, most of them ex-cons, many of them killers convicted and otherwise. The gangs that controlled the crack cocaine trade were lethal, but for the most part they preyed on each other; their outside victims were usually innocent bystanders who happened to get in the way of a stray drive-by bullet. The crystal meth bunch were even more lethal, the difference being that they had a reputation for indiscriminate slaughter. Anybody who crossed them or got in their way, for any reason, was fair game.

Baldy wasn't Jackie Spoons. Jackie was too big, too tall, and the last time I'd set eyes on him he'd worn a thick Fu Manchu mustache and had a pile of wavy black hair. He wouldn't have needed a gun to do the job on me, either. He'd have gotten me in a chokehold and snapped my neck with one quick twist. He had arms like Popeye's and hands like catcher's gloves. Jackie Shovels would have been a more appropriate sobriquet. But the name Spoons hadn't come from the size of his hands; it was a childhood nickname pinned on him because his father, a Greek immigrant and amateur musician, had made music with ordinary spoons and tried to teach his son to do the same. Jackie's real name was something like Andropopolous.

Nick Kinsella. I knew him a little; he wasn't Baldy, either. He owned a place on San Bruno Avenue, off Bayshore west of Candlestick Park, called the Blacklight Tavern, but that wasn't his primary source of income. He'd made his pile in the time-honored trade of loan-sharking. Another rough-trader: he charged a heavy weekly vig, and if you missed a payment or two you could expect a visit from one of his enforcers—big, bad boys like Jackie Spoons. Once, years ago, I'd tracked down and brought back a bail-jumper for a bondsman named Abe Melikian. The jumper was somebody Kinsella had a grudge against; he liked me for putting the guy back in the slammer. Any time I needed a favor, he'd said to me at the time. I'd taken him up on it once, when I had no other way to get certain information. Maybe my credit was still good for one more favor.

I drove south on Bayshore, took the San Bruno Avenue exit. This was one of the city's older residential neighborhoods, workingclass like the one I'd grown up in in the Outer Mission. During World War II, and while the Hunters Point Naval Shipyard humped along for twenty-five years afterward, it had been a reasonably decent section in which to live and raise a family. Then the shipyard shut down, the mostly black wartime work force stayed on, and a variety of factors, not the least of which were poverty and racism, combined to erode Hunters Point into a mean-streets ghetto. Now, with the crack-infested Point on one side and the drug deli that McLaren Park had become on the other, this neighborhood had eroded, too. Signs of decay were everywhere: boarded-up store-fronts, bars on windows and doors, houses defaced by graffiti and neglect, homeless people and drunks huddled in doorways.

The Blacklight Tavern fit right in. It was aptly named: From a distance the building looked like one that had been badly scorched in a fire. Black-painted facade, smoke-tinted windows, black sign with neon letters that would blaze white after dark but seemed burned out in the daylight. I parked down the block and locked the car, not that that would stop anybody who thought it might contain something tradeable for a rock of crack or a jug of cheap sweet wine.

Inside, the place might have been O'Key's or any other bottom-feeder bar populated by the usual array of late-afternoon drinkers. Two hustlers, one black and one white, gave me bleary-eyed once-overs as I moved up to the bar. The bartender had a head like a redwood burl and a surly manner. All he said when I caught his eye was, "Yeah?"

"Nick Kinsella. He in?"

"Who's asking?"

I passed over one of my business cards. He didn't even glance at it.

"Mr. Kinsella know you?"

"He knows me. Tell him it's a business matter."

"Be a few minutes, maybe. Drink while you're waiting?"

"Beer. Whatever you have on draft."

He drew the beer, slid it over, and took my card to a back-bar phone.

The white hustler, a chubby blonde in her middle thirties, came sidling over and rubbed a meaty breast against my arm. "Big," she said. Whiskey voice, as deep as a man's. "Big all over, I'll bet."

"You'll never know," I said.

"Oh, now, don't be like that. Be friendly. This is a friendly place. Buy me a drink?"

"I'm here on business."

"So am I, honey. Buy me a drink?"

"No."

"One little drink, just to be friendly."

"I said no. I'm not interested in company."

"Buy the lady a drink, for Chrissakes," somebody behind me said. "What the hell?"

I turned halfway to look. He was young, wearing the stained overalls and cap of a painter; the looseness in his face and the shine in his eyes said he'd been here awhile. He wasn't alone in his afternoon bag. He had a friend, similarly dressed, similarly red-faced, perched on the stool next to him.

"What the hell *you* lookin' at, Pops?" the same one said.

Terrific. Another small man with a small mind, the kind of two-brain-cell cretin who turns mean and belligerent on an alcohol diet and looks for an excuse to flex his bloated machismo. I turned away from him without answering. Anything I said would have been provocative.

"Hey, I ask you a question."

The other one had some sense left. He said, "Let him 'lone, Marty. We don't want no trouble."

"I ask him a question." Hard and tough. He poked my elbow and said, "Hey, you old fuck, I ask you a question. Why don't you answer me, huh?"

Old fuck. The same thing Baldy had called me last night. I could hear the clicks again, loud and clear. And the rage that surged into my throat was so sudden and virulent it surprised me; I had to almost literally hold it down, using the beveled edge of the bar and both hands as a surrogate.

"Let him 'lone, Marty, goddamn it."

"Old fuck comes in here, gives me a look, don't answer me when I talk to him. Who's he think he is?"

Back off, I thought. Back off!

No. He said, "Hey, lookit, he's marked up. Somebody else dint like his looks. Hey, Pops, you want some more marks on that ugly face of yours?"

I turned again, even more slowly, and faced him square on. It was an effort to keep my voice even when I said, "I've had enough of your bullshit. Mind your own business."

"What you say to me?"

"You heard what I said. You don't want any part of me, Marty. Not now, not ever. Start something and you'll crawl out of here bleeding. Guaranteed."

He made a bullish noise and started clumsily off his stool. The other one caught his arm, held him down. "Jesus," he said, "Jesus, Marty, he means it. Lookit his face. He means it."

The bartender was back. He said, "He's not the only one means it," and he leaned over and cuffed Marty on the side of the head, not lightly.

The blow caught the drunk by surprise; it also confused him. He blinked half a dozen times, rubbing his head. "Hey, Pete, what's the idea, hah?"

"Shut up. Stick your nose in your drink and keep it there, you know what's good for you."

"Sure. Sure, I doan want no hassle with you, Pete." He aimed one last weak glare my way, then hunched down and wrapped both hands around his glass. Pouting now, with his lower lip poked out like a three-year-old. He wasn't seeing anybody or anything except his own alcoholic haze.

"Okay," the bartender said to me in a different, almost respectful tone. "Nick'll see you. First door past the ladies' crapper."

"I've been here before."

"I ain't surprised."

I went back there, conscious of eyes following me, and knocked on the door and walked into a mostly barren office that stank of cigar smoke and fried food. It had two men in it, Kinsella and a lop-sided, three-hundred-pound giant with a heavy five-o'clock shadow and a gold earring that gave him the look of a dim-witted pirate. One of the shark's enforcers, no doubt. Kinsella sat bulging behind a cherrywood desk. He had three chins and a waistline as big as the giant's, though he was seven or eight inches shorter. The two of them wore grease on their mouths and fingers, courtesy of a bucket of fast-food fried chicken squatting on the desk.

I shut the door behind me. "Long time, Nick."

"Long time," he agreed. "You want some chicken? We got plenty. Extra-crispy."

"No, thanks. Not hungry."

"Wish I could say the same. I got the curse—I'm always hungry." He hoisted a wad of soiled paper towel off his lap, wiped his fingers and dabbed almost delicately at his mouth. "I won't ask how you been. I figure I know the answer. I figure I got a pretty good idea why you come around to see me."

"Is that right?"

"I read four papers every day," he said, "watch the TV news every night. I like to know what's going on. You come close to it last night, my friend."

"Yeah," I said. "Close."

"I'm relieved it's only close. I don't like funerals, and I figure I'd've had to go to yours out of respect."

"I guess I should be flattered."

"Nah. I don't like funerals but I go to a lot of 'em because I know a lot of people that die sudden." He pulled a chicken leg out of the bucket, tore off a chunk of meat with teeth so white and perfect they had to be implants. "Go ahead, eat, Bluto," he said to the giant. "You don't have to stand there like a lump with drool on your mouth."

The giant helped himself. Chewing, Kinsella said to me, "Bluto ain't his real name. I call him that on account of he reminds me of the guy in Popeye. You sure you don't want some chicken?"

"Positive."

"So anyway, I figure you want me to tell you something, but I can't figure what it is. You got to know nobody in my organization would pull a stunt like that one last night. Hijacking cash and killing schoolteachers, that ain't my business or my style."

"I know it's not."

"So?"

"So the police aren't the only ones looking for the shooter. Big guy about forty, bald, bushy eyebrows, onion breath. Uses a short-barreled revolver, likely a thirty-eight."

"Could be anybody. How come you figure I'd know him?"

"You know a lot of people, like you said."

"Not somebody looks like that. You, Bluto?"

Bluto's mouth was full of chicken breast; he grunted and shook his head.

"So," Kinsella said, "I figure there's something else you want me to tell you. Some other angle. Like maybe you figure this bald schmuck wasn't a solo worker. Like maybe you figure the lady's husband was in on it."

"You're pretty sharp, Nick."

"Sure I am. That's how come I'm still in business after, what, twenty-three years. That's how come I pay such high taxes." He finished the chicken leg, threw the bone into his wastebasket. Cleaned his fingers and his mouth again, tossed the greasy paper towels in with the bones, and fired up one of the black stogies he favored. Two puffs, and the air grayed; I could feel congestion form in my chest. "Cohalan, that's the husband's name, right? I don't know him, neither."

"He's a crankhead," I said. "He's got a girlfriend who's a crankhead. There's a chance the two of them were dealing as well as using, that that's what they wanted the money for."

"So? That also ain't my business."

"No, but I hear it's Jackie Spoons' business now."

"Aha," he said. "So that's it. Jackie Spoons."

"I know he doesn't work for you anymore, but I thought you might know where I can find him."

"He's crazy, you know that? A crazy man."

"Crazy enough for hijacking and murder?"

"Sure, but not the way it was done last night. Uh-uh."

"I just want to talk to him."

"When he quit me," Kinsella said, "I was glad to see him go. He don't take orders, he don't show restraint, he don't act like a normal human being. And he don't like to talk to people he don't know."

"I won't cross him."

"Maybe you don't think so. But what you call crossing and what he calls crossing might be two different things. You come close to it last night. I'd hate to see your luck run out with Jackie Spoons, and I have to go to your funeral after all."

"That won't happen. Where can I find him, Nick?"

He sucked on his stogie, blew a stream of foul-smelling smoke in my direction. I coughed and waved it away, but he didn't seem to notice. "Well, what the hell. I said my piece. I figure you don't want to listen to good advice, that's your business. I figure maybe you're entitled to push your luck. I might push mine, too, if I'd been the one come close to it in Daly City."

"I'll keep your name out of it. He won't know where I got the information."

"You figure I care about that? I don't care about that. Jackie Spoons is crazy, but he don't scare me. Nobody scares me except Uncle Sam. That's why I pay my high taxes right on time every year, don't take no questionable deductions." He sent another spurt of smoke my way. "Okay. You know the Veterans' Gym? Out near the Daly City line?"

"I know it. That's my old neighborhood."

"Yeah? The Outer Mission?"

"Born and raised."

"I be damned," Kinsella said. "I didn't know that. Used to be a good, solid working-class neighborhood. Now it's as shitty as this one. Whole damn city's falling apart, you ask me."

And you're one of those who helped with the deconstruction, I thought. I said, "The Veterans' Gym where Jackie Spoons hangs out?"

"That's where. Lifts weights, watches the pissants that pass for fighters these days train—like that."

"Do his dealing there, too?"

"Uh-uh. He's crazy, but he's smart enough not to crap where he relaxes. You go out there, ask for Zeke Mayjack. Him and Jackie Spoons been friends a long time. You connect with Zeke, schmooz him a little, get him to walk you up to his buddy, and maybe Jackie'll talk to you after all."

"Thanks, Nick."

"Don't thank me yet. You ain't seen Jackie Spoons yet."

I said, "Before I leave, can I run a couple more names by you?"

His sigh turned into a hacking cough. When he got it under control he said, "These names maybe also connected?"

"Maybe. I'll know when I find them."

"So go ahead."

"Charlie Bright. Junkie and small-time dealer."

"Nah. Bluto?"

Bluto shook his head.

"Dingo," I said.

"What the hell kind of name is that, Dingo?"

"I don't know that it is somebody's name. A place, maybe. Mean anything?"

"Nah. Bluto?"

Bluto shook his head.

"So that's it then," I said. "Unless I can talk you into asking around about Bright and Dingo?"

He thought about it. "I did you one favor, now you figure I'm good for more than one in return. Well, maybe I am. I'm a soft touch for people I like, people done me a good turn one time. But I'm also a guy believes in what you call your quid pro quo. You done me a favor, I done you a couple, now I figure we're even. So if I ask around about this Bright and this Dingo, then I figure you owe me one. Not right away, but someday, and you don't say no when I ask. Fair enough?"

I didn't like the idea of being in Nick Kinsella's debt, but I did not have much choice. If I refused it would offend him, and Kinsella was nobody you wanted to be mad at you. "Fair enough," I said.

He grinned, coughed, scowled, jabbed the stogie into an ashtray, and grinned again. "I got your card, I'll call you. Won't be too long, one way or the other." I nodded and turned for the door, and he said, "And don't forget what I told you."

"About the quid pro quo?"

"Nah. About Jackie Spoons being crazy. About don't make me have to go to your funeral after all."

The Veterans' Gym was one of those time-warp places that have somehow managed to survive into the technological age and the new millenium. One good reason, if not the only one, is that it was tucked away in a blue-collar section well removed from the heart of the city. Even so, its days had to be numbered. San Francisco's explosive economy has driven real estate values through the roof and changed the city's shape, cultural diversity, and future. It used to be a bohemian paradise, flavored by old-world ethnicity and a laissez-faire attitude; now, the bohemians and artists, poor by nature, are being forced out in droves, and residential and commercial space is being auctioned off to the highest bidder. Big Business and Big Bucks rule, and you can't tell the politicans from the developers and all the other high-profile, high-living, high-handed movers and shakers. The old way of San Francisco life is dying; places like the Veterans' Gym, despite its location, are little more than upright corpses waiting for the undertaker.

As soon as I walked in, it was like stepping back fifty years or more—into a scene in a circa 1950 black-and-white boxing flick that had been poorly colorized. The walls in the big anteroom were coated with fight cards, many of them for bouts that had been held in the old Civic Auditorium, and high-gloss photos of boxers in fighting poses. A lot of the names were familiar: Joe Louis, Ezzard Charles. Unfamiliar were such long-gone, long-forgotten local white hopes as Silent Ramponi and Mongo "The Rock" Luciano. Through an open doorway I could see part of the main gym, two guys sparring in a ring, somebody in sweats banging away on a light bag. Smack of leather on leather, male voices yelling encouragements and obscenities. Smells of sweat and liniment and leather and canvas and wood so old even the termites were fifth or sixth generation. Strictly a male domain, the Veterans'. Not even the most ardent feminist would care to try breaching its testosterone-soaked atmosphere.

A counter ran along the wall next to the gym entrance, and behind it was a guy about my age whose torso bulged in a light sweatshirt with the word *Veterans'* across the front. Ex-light heavyweight, from the look of him. He gave me the once-over as I approached and was not impressed: I had the wrong look, the wrong body type, and I was a stranger besides.

He said, "Do something?" in a voice like rocks being shaken in a can. Hit in the throat hard enough once, I thought, to damage his windpipe and vocal chords.

"Zeke Mayjack around?"

"Who wants him?"

I told him who. The name didn't impress him, either.

"I don't know you," he said. "Zeke know you?"

"No. I'm a friend of a friend."

"Yeah?"

"Nick Kinsella."

Nothing changed in his face, but he said, "Zeke ain't here."

"Expect him any time soon?"

Shrug. "He comes and goes."

"Best time to catch him is when?"

"He comes and goes, like I told you."

"Any idea where he might be now?"

"No."

And if he knew where Zeke Mayjack lived, he wouldn't tell me. I asked, "How about Jackie Spoons? He around?"

"Who?"

"Jackie Spoons."

"Never heard of him."

Yeah, I thought, just like you never hard of Marciano or Ali. But there was nothing to be gained in pushing it. Kinsella's name was good enough for an introduction to Mayjack, but I'd have to go through Mayjack to get to Jackie Spoons. That told me something about Jackie's standing at the Veterans': hands-off unless you were known to the staff and cleared for an audience. Money, fear? That combination, and also the closed-circle attitude you found in old clubs like this one. Whatever else Jackie Spoons was, he was also one of their gym rats.

Nothing else for me here right now. I could hang around and wait for Mayjack, but it could turn into a long wait, and I was not up to it. It was already six o'clock, and I was tired of the urban jungle, tired of walking the edges. Enough for today.

I thought about going to my flat in Pacific Heights, as I had told Kerry I might do. The flat, which I had occupied on a rent-controlled lease for more than three decades, had been a good place to live when I was single, a good place to hole up in sad, bad times then and since. Most of my pulp magazine collection was there, and a lot of my other long-time possessions. Since I'd gotten settled into marriage, though, it had begun to feel less and less like home, and I did not go there nearly as often. Maybe the time had come to give it up, move the pulps to the condo and the rest of my stuff into storage. I hadn't been able to take that step yet, but I had the sense that I would be ready to before much longer. I felt it again now because I did not really want to go to the flat tonight, did not really want to be alone there or anywhere.

Home was the condo, home was Kerry and Emily. I went home.

12

EMILY HUGGED ME FIERCELY WHEN I WALKED IN, but afterward she withdrew again into her self-protective shell. She was very quiet during dinner, ate almost nothing, refused desert, and went straight to her room.

Kerry had been demonstrative enough at the table, trying to draw Emily out, but she grew quiet when we were alone. There was something she wanted to say to me, only she was not quite ready to say it. Just as well. I could guess what it was and I was not quite ready to hear it.

We cleaned up and then sat in the living room and made desultory conversation. Not about where I'd been or what I'd been doing all day; she didn't ask and I didn't volunteer any information. That was something else I was not yet ready to discuss. The main topic was Cybil. Kerry and her mother had had a long phone talk about what had happened, and Cybil had offered to take Emily for a few days until things "calmed down." Kerry thought it might be a good idea; I didn't. Cybil was eighty and lived in a seniors' complex, but that wasn't the main reason I objected. The kid had been displaced enough in the past year. It wouldn't do her or us any good if she were uprooted in the midst of a new crisis. She had to learn to deal with life's calamities large and small, not to run or hide from them, and sheltering her was not the way for the lesson to be taught.

So we hashed it out, and Kerry finally agreed with me. But then she said, "I think you'd better talk to her about last night. I tried, but I can't get through to her. It has to come from you."

"Now, tonight?"

"Right now. She knows we almost lost you. She was there; she saw the way you looked . . . she's not dealing with it very well."

None of us are, I thought. And you were there, too, babe. I said, "Maybe I'd better. Get it out into the open."

"It would be best."

For us, too. But I didn't say it.

I went and knocked on Emily's door and put my head inside. She was in bed, propped up against the pillows, Shameless curled and purring beside her, one of her dozen or so stuffed animals—a grinning Garfield—clutched against her chest. All the lights were on: overheads and bedside lamp in there, ceiling and vanity lights in the adjoining bathroom.

"Okay if I come in?"

"Yes."

I shut the door and sat at the foot of her bed. "Kind of bright in here, kiddo. Too much light for sleeping."

"I can't sleep. I don't want to."

"Why not?"

"Bad dreams."

"What kind of bad dreams?"

"Ugly . . . the ugly kind. I don't want to talk about them."

"You might feel better if you did."

"No." She grimaced, put her hand on Shameless as if for warmth and comfort. He licked her finger, purred louder. "I think there's something wrong with me," she said.

"Wrong? Don't you feel well?"

"That's not what I mean. I mean with *me*, the person I am."

"There's nothing wrong with you, honey. Why would you think that?"

"You know."

"No, I don't."

"Everybody keeps dying," she said. "Everybody I care about. Dad, Mom . . . everybody."

I could feel her pain; it was my pain, too. I said, "I'm still here. I didn't die last night."

"You almost did. When I came in that house and saw you . . . all the blood . . . I thought you were going to. That's the first thing I thought." A shudder went through her. "I'm still afraid you're going to."

Dead man walking.

Click. Click.

I kept it out of my face, or tried to. She was looking at me the way a kid can sometimes, penetratingly and with a depth of intuition and understanding no adult can match. She knows, I thought. She's known all along.

What I said to her now was more important than anything I'd ever said to her. No simplistic, homespun philosophy of the sort I'd dished out at the zoo on Friday; something with heft and meaning and impact. I framed it in my head, found a way to begin, and plunged in.

"You must think you're pretty special, Emily."

"I'm not special—"

"Powerful, too. A special, powerful little girl."

"I don't think that. I'm not."

"As special and powerful as God. A kind of god yourself."

The words shocked her, as I'd intended them to. She sat upright, her face all rounded O's—eyes, mouth, flared nostrils. "That's not true!"

"No? Then how can you believe you cause people to die? God's the only being who can do that, not that I believe He does. So if you can do it you must have godlike powers yourself. Right?"

"No! It's not like that. It's . . . they die because of me, something in me. . . ."

"That doesn't make any sense. Unless you believe you're evil instead of godlike. Is that how you see yourself? An evil person?"

"I'm not that, either. . . . I'm *not*."

"Of course you're not. You're neither godlike nor evil. You're a ten-year-old girl named Emily Hunter who's had a lot of bad things happen to her and to people she loves—things that aren't her fault. Not hers, not God's, not anybody's. You didn't make them happen. You didn't have anything to do with them happening."

"Then why did they happen?"

"Some people would say it's God's will. I don't buy that. I think God's an observer, not an active participant; I think He pretty much stays out of human business. I think bad things happen because there are bad people in the world and sometimes good people get in the way. There's no reason or purpose to it—it's random, accidental. You understand?"

"Yes, but . . . then what's the use of praying?"

"It makes you feel better, doesn't it? Closer to God?"

" . . . I suppose so."

"It helps you, that's the point. Divine miracles are few and far between, Emily. The only miracles most of us get are the ones we bring to ourselves."

"By being good people, leading good lives?"

"That's right."

"But people we care about still die." She hugged Garfield closer. "I can't help it, I'm still afraid."

"You're not alone. So am I."

"Of dying?"

"No. Everybody dies sooner or later. Dying's pretty easy when you get right down to it. Living's the hard part."

"What are you scared of, then?"

"Of what will happen to you if I die before you grow up. Not so much where you'd go or what you'd do, but how you'd be inside.

That you'd always be afraid. That you might never have a life because you're too concerned with death. That scares me more than anything. More than you're scared right now."

She gave me a long, searching look. And then, all at once, she began to cry. Fat tears and low, hard-wrung sobs, as if an emotional dam had burst deep within her. And that was good, as painful as it was to watch, because it was the first time her grief and pain had come pouring out in front of me or Kerry or anyone else.

I ached to hold her, comfort her—but not yet, not until the purge was finished. I just sat there, feeling bad-good for her and mostly bad for myself.

When I came out I told Kerry about it, and she agreed that the breakdown was a positive sign. She went in to see Emily herself, to offer comfort and to reinforce what I'd said. And when she came out—

"She's better now. I think she'll be able to sleep tonight."

"She let you turn off the lights?"

"All except the nightlight in the bathroom."

Another good sign. If Emily was able to deal with one kind of darkness now, in time she'd probably learn to deal with the other kind.

A little later Kerry and I went to bed. We lay quietly, holding hands. I wanted to talk to her as freely as I'd talked to Emily, but with Kerry it would mean reliving the near-death experience, and my emotional dam on that subject was still tightly closed. I sensed that she was ready to speak her piece, though, and I was right.

Pretty soon she said, "There's something I need to say. I don't want to preach at you, or try to tell you what to do, but you have to understand how I feel."

"Go ahead."

"I'm not so different from Emily," she said. "Last night . . . it scared me, too. We came so close to losing you."

"Close only counts in horseshoes."

"Dammit, this isn't funny."

"I wasn't trying to be funny."

"You could be dead right now."

"I know that better than you do."

"Yes, all right. I didn't mean . . . I don't know what I meant. I suppose I'm being selfish, but I can't help being afraid for myself and for Emily, as well as for you."

"That's not selfish, just human."

"We can't go through something like this again," she said. "None of us can, you most of all."

"Quit beating around the bush. Just say it."

"All right. I think it's time you . . . cut back. Stop putting yourself in situations where you can get hurt or killed."

"Retire, you mean. Get out of the detective business."

"I didn't say that."

"It's what you meant."

"No, it isn't, not exactly. Cut back, take a less active role in the agency. Give Tamara more responsibility, hire somebody else to do the fieldwork."

"Somebody younger."

"Age isn't the issue here."

"Isn't it?"

" . . . Okay, maybe it is, partly. You're sixty years old—"

"You think sixty's old?"

"No, sixty is not old. Not in the normal course of things. But when it comes to dangerous situations, physical abuse . . . you can't keep on doing the things you did twenty or thirty years ago, taking the kind of beating you took last night. You know you can't."

I didn't say anything.

"You know you can't," she said again.

Lay still, you old fuck. Hey, Pops, you want some more marks on that ugly face of yours? Hey, you old fuck.

"And now you're out there again," Kerry said, "prowling around on the mean streets or whatever you call them, doing God knows what that might get you hurt again or killed this time.

Don't tell me that's not what you were doing today. I know better. I know you."

I let that pass as well.

"You have to stop this before it's too late."

"Not yet."

"Why not, for God's sake?"

"If you know me so well, you know the answer to that."

"The hunter, always the hunter. Hemingway bullshit. Macho bullshit."

"It's not bullshit. Not for me. And I'm not hunting the way you mean."

"No?"

"No. I'm after justice, not revenge."

"Fine, but you're still out there, still vulnerable."

"I know what I'm doing," I said.

"Famous last words. Can't you understand I need you, Emily needs you—alive, safe?"

"I understand a lot better than you think."

"But still you won't quit."

"Not until my client's murderer is identified and caught."

"And when he is, if he is, what then?"

Give up my flat, give up my job . . . give up my life. Or was it giving up? Or just adapting, changing, accepting more important responsibilities, moving on to a different phase of my life?

"I don't know," I said. "Maybe you're right."

"I am right. Will you at least think about it?"

"Yes. All right, yes, I'll think about it."

Sunday morning, a few minutes past nine, the phone rang. I answered it, thinking that it might be Tamara with new information. No. The call was for me, but the voice on the other end belonged to Lieutenant John Fuentes, Daly City PD.

"Glad I caught you in," he said in a voice that didn't sound glad about anything. "You free this morning?"

"Yes. Why?"

"Appreciate it if you'd meet me at the Hall of Justice. Say in about an hour."

"You mean here in the city?"

"We don't have a Hall of Justice in Daly City." Testy now. Nobody likes working Sunday mornings. "Coroner's office, one hour."

"Coroner's office?"

"We're going to look at a body found in an abandoned car earlier this morning, see if you can identify it. Victim of homicide, evidently."

"Why me?"

"One good reason," Fuentes said. "The abandoned car belongs to Jay Cohalan."

13

THE DEAD MAN IN THE REFRIGERATED MORGUE locker had been badly used before he was murdered. Facial bruises, nose broken, upper lip split in two places. Beaten and then, at some point, shot in the back of the head. The body lay face up so the entrance wound wasn't visible, but the ragged hole below the right eye was plainly an exit wound.

The two cops stood watching me from the other side of the sliding table. A study in contrasts, those two. Lieutenant John Fuentes was a little guy, stringy, in his early fifties, slow-moving and deliberate, wearing a perpetual half-smile that hid a suspicious mind and an abrasive personality. The mole on his cheek was the size of a garbanzo bean; I wondered irrelevently if there was much risk of it becoming cancerous. Inspector Harry Craddock, SFPD Homicide, was a broad-beamed black man pushing forty, eight inches taller than Fuentes, fidgety standing or sitting, serious-meined and dedicated to the point of obsession—your classic Type A. I'd had dealings with Craddock before and we'd always gotten along. Fuentes was another matter. It was obvious he'd taken a dislike to me, for

whatever reason; every time he aimed a question or comment my
way, the words seemed underscored with accusation and grated on
me like sandpaper.

He said when I lifted my head, "Well?"

"Jay Cohalan."

"Uh-huh. What we figured."

"No ID on him?"

"Would I have called you if there was?"

"Why did you call me? Must be somebody else who could have
ID'ed the body."

"Why do you think?"

"I don't know anything about this."

"No?"

"No."

Craddock said, "Let's continue this upstairs." He chafed his
hands together, blew into them. "It's too goddamn cold down here."

He gestured to the coroner's attendant, who slid what was left of
Cohalan back into the locker, and the three of us went out to the
elevators. Craddock's office was in the main Hall of Justice
building, second floor. On the way there we passed an alcove of
vending machines; he stopped, saying, "I can use a cup of coffee."
Fuentes didn't want anything. Neither did I.

"Christ, I hate going to the morgue." Craddock again, when we
were settled around his desk. Both his big hands were wrapped
tight around the foam cup of hot coffee. "Chill down there goes
right to your bones."

"Didn't seem cold to me," Fuentes said.

Craddock tipped him a look. "Maybe your blood's thicker than
mine."

"Maybe it is. You know how hot-blooded us Latinos are."
Craddock didn't bite on that, and the false half-smile swung my
way. "So you don't know anything about what happened to
Cohalan?"

"That's right. The last time I saw him or talked to him was

Thursday night at Annette Byers' apartment. How long has he been dead?"

"Coroner's estimate is minimum of thirty-six hours," Craddock answered.

Fuentes said, "Killed sometime Friday night, before or after the Carolyn Dain homicide and the attempt on you. Probably after."

I had no comment on that.

"Who do you think killed him?"

"Pretty obvious, isn't it? Shot execution style the same as Ms. Dain." The same as me. Click. Click. "If the slug was recovered, Ballistics'll prove it came from the same gun."

"We've got it," Craddock said. "It was inside the trunk of the car. Looks like Cohalan was stuffed in there alive and then shot."

"Where was the car?"

"Out near Candlestick. Security patrol spotted it and called us. Trunk lid was up—somebody'd jimmied it open, neighborhood kids or adults, and then run like hell when they saw what was inside."

"Any sign of Byers?"

"No. Nothing in the car but the corpse."

"Prints?"

"Wiped clean."

"Whose car?"

"Registered to Cohalan. Three-year-old Camry."

Why did Baldy take his wallet, then? I wondered. Confuse the issue, possibly, make it look like a robbery homicide. He might've wanted Cohalan's credit cards, too. Baldy was a greed-driven psycho, and not very smart; a walletful of credit cards could be an irresistable temptation to a man like that.

Fuentes asked me, with that suspicious edge in his voice, "You know Annette Byers—where does she fit into this?"

"I don't know her. I've only spoken to her the one time."

"Accessory or victim?"

"Could be either one."

"That's not an answer."

"Look, Lieutenant, I don't know any more about this than you do. Why pick on me?"

"Make a guess about Byers."

"What good is guesswork?"

"Make a guess," he said.

I held onto my temper. "Okay, a guess. Accessory. Mixed up with the bald man in some way."

"Lovers?"

"Maybe."

"She was screwing Cohalan, wasn't she?"

"Evidently."

"Well?"

"What do you want me to say? That maybe she was working with Baldy all along, just using Cohalan to get hold of the seventy-five thousand? That he found out the truth and squawked, and that's why he was murdered? It could've happened that way. But it's just one possible scenario."

"And you can't identify the bald man."

"If I could, I'd've done it Friday night."

"No idea where he and the woman might be?"

"Same answer."

"You wouldn't be having notions, would you?"

"Meaning what?"

"You know what. The personal, payback kind."

Too close to home. The smart thing for me to do would be to give him and Craddock everything I'd come up with so far—Steve Niall, Charlie Bright, Jackie Spoons, the Dingo message, the plastic "Remember the Alamo!" chip. But I'd known coming in here that I was not likely to play it smart, and nothing I'd seen or heard had changed my mind. I didn't like Fuentes or his attitude any more than he cared for me or mine, and besides, all I really had were possibilities and conjecture—no direct link to Baldy or Byers or the missing money or the two murders. Withholding evidence is a criminal act; withholding prospective knowledge is a nonactionable sin of omission.

I said, "You're way off base, Lieutenant."

"I'd better be."

"I've cooperated so far—I'll continue to cooperate. The only thing you should know that I haven't already told you is that there's a probable drug connection in all this."

That bent his smile out of shape. "What kind of drug connection?"

"Cohalan was a crankhead; so is Byers. They were stoned before and after I took the money away from them Thursday night. I figure Baldy's cut from the same cloth—user, supplier, or both."

"I didn't see anything in your case file about drugs."

"It wasn't germane to the job I was hired to do. Carolyn Dain knew her husband was using, but she didn't tell me about it up front. I found out in the course of my investigation."

"Why didn't you report this to me before now?"

"I would have if I'd been thinking clearly. Almost getting killed has a way of making you forgetful, among other things."

"Damn straight," Craddock said. "Ease up on him, John. He's as much a victim here as the two morgue cases."

"That doesn't earn him any special favors."

"He's cooperating, isn't he? Like he said?" There was an edge in Craddock's tone. Fuentes' suspicious nature was wearing thin on him, too. "Cut him some slack."

"You know him better than I do," Fuentes said, and got to his feet. He glanced at Craddock, then fixed his gaze on me. "I'll be in touch."

"I'm sure you will."

"Count on it. See you, Harry."

Craddock gestured but didn't answer. When Fuentes was gone, he took his time lighting one of the plastic-mouthpiece cigarillos he favored. The no-smoking-in-public-places law didn't seem to be in force here in the bosom of the law, any more than it was in O'Key's saloon.

He said through a gout of smoke, "Fuentes doesn't seem to like you much."

"I noticed."

"By-the-book type. Ex-military. Keeps his ass clenched so tight he could crack nuts between his cheeks."

"He has no cause to want to crack mine."

"What I figured. Cooperating, like you said."

"Like I said. Haven't I always?"

"With me you have. So if you turned up some definite information on the Cohalan homicide, just happened to stumble across it, say, you'd let me know."

"Before I even thought about contacting Fuentes."

Craddock grinned a little. He understood what was going on with me, all right. He had qualities of empathy, humanity, insight that had been short-supplied to the good lieutenant. "I asked him for a copy of your Cohalan file. Said he'd get me one, but I got a feeling he'll make me wait for it."

"I can give you the gist of it right now. And put a copy in your hands first thing tomorrow morning."

"Tomorrow's soon enough. I got plenty of other open cases to keep me busy today." Craddock picked up his cup, sipped from it, pulled a face that said the coffee had gotten cold. He frowned at the cup, frowned at his cigarillo. "I hate working Sundays," he said.

"Everybody does. Not much choice, sometimes."

"Yeah. Well, suppose you slide on outta here, and we'll both get on with it."

A different guy was manning the counter at Veterans' Gym—musclebound, tight-mouthed, and bored. When I asked if Zeke Mayjack was around, he jerked a thumb toward the main gym entrance without even looking at me. I said, "Okay to go in?" and he scowled and jerked the thumb again. The owners of the Veterans' seemed to have a knack for hiring the personality challenged.

Late Sunday morning appeared to be a slow time here. Of the seven people I counted in the gym, only three were getting exercise—a grunting welterweight giving the big bag a workout and two light-heavies in headgear and sweats thumping each other in the ring. A tired-looking fat man leaned against the ropes in one corner, issuing instructions in a monotone that the sluggers paid no attention to. A pair of hard-eyed characters was hanging close outside the ring, giving more heed to each other than to the sparring partners. Beyond where they stood, a grizzled old man sat on a three-legged stool, yelling sporadic advice to one of the sluggers who also ignored him. His raised voice and the smack of leather against flesh had an echolike effect in the cavernous enclosure.

I made a guess and approached the hard-eyed pair. Wrong guess. One of them said, "Mayjack? That's him on the stool over there."

Zeke Mayjack was not what I'd expected in more ways than one. Mid-seventies, sparse white hair like a curly skullcap, of indeterminate race: he might have been white, or mixed blood, or a fair-skinned African American. Probably a light-heavy in his days, like the pair in the ring, and not a very good one judging from his bent, flattened, lumpy features. One eye had gone milky with cataracts—blind, or close to it. The other had the shiny stare common to scramble-brained ex-pugs who've taken too many hard blows above the neck.

"Keep your head down, baby," he was hollering as I walked up. "Down, man, *down*, goddamn it."

"Zeke Mayjack, right?" I said. "Talk to you for a minute?"

The one good eye shifted my way, slid over the marks on my face. A cackling sound that had a hitch and a hiss in it came out of him. "Man, you shoulda kept your head down, too. Cut you up if you don't."

I let that pass and told him my name. That was as far as I got.

"Yeah," he said. "Yeah, I been waiting on you. He says he don't want to see you, he don't have nothing to say to you."

"Who doesn't want to see me?"

"Hey, who else? Jackie."

"Jackie Spoons?"

"You know some other Jackie, honey boy?"

"How'd he know I want to talk to him?"

"He knows. Yeah, he knows everything," The cackle again. "He's like Sanny Claus."

Sanny Claus. Christ. "Why won't he talk to me?"

"Jackie, he says tell you you're barkin' up the wrong tree. He says he don't know a fuckin' thing about it."

"About what?"

Shrug.

"Jay Cohalan? Carolyn Dain?"

Shrug. The one good eye wandered ringward. "Get that left up, for cry sake. C'mon, Frankie, you punk, jab. Yeah, that's the way. Jab, jab, head down, jab."

"What else did Jackie say?"

"Huh?"

"What else did he say to tell me?"

"Oh, yeah. Don't hassle him if you know what's good for you. Stay away from him if you know what's good for you. Better do what he says. Cut you up a lot worse if you get Jackie pissed off. Lot worse, man,"

"Is that all?"

"All?"

"His message. That all of it?"

"Yeah." The good eye blinked; the blind one stared glassily from under a lid enlarged by scar tissue. "No, it ain't. Jackie says go talk to that fuckin' Aussie."

"What Aussie?"

Shrug.

"Dingo? That who he meant?"

"Yeah, him. Jackie don't like him, honey boy."

"Why doesn't Jackie like him?"

Shrug.

"He do something to Jackie?"

"Nah. Nobody does nothing to Jackie."

"What's he look like?"

"Who? Jackie?"

"Dingo. The Aussie."

"Yeah, what about him?"

"What does he look like? Big, bald, bushy eyebrows?"

"I don't know him, baby," Mayjack said.

"You mean you've never seen him?"

"Nah. He don't come around here."

"What's his real name? Dingo's real name?"

Shrug.

"I can't go talk to him if I don't know where to find him. Come on, Zeke, you must have some idea—"

"Hey, hey, man, my friends call me Zeke and you ain't my friend. I don't know you. You call me Mr. Mayjack."

"Where do I look for Dingo, Mr. Mayjack?"

Shrug. Then, explosively, "Goddamn it! Shit!" as a flurry of loud smacks came from the ring, and one of the light-heavies bounced on the canvas. "I told you head down, left up, *up*. Smart-ass young punk, why don't you listen?"

"I'm listening," I said.

"Huh?"

"Dingo, Mr. Mayjack."

"Jackie don't like that fuckin' Aussie. That's what he said. I don't like that fuckin' Aussie, Zeke, he said."

"They in the same business? Is that why Jackie doesn't like him?"

Mayjack's face clouded; his mouth pinched in at the corners. "Don't ask me about that, honey boy. Boxing's my business. Yeah. Jackie's business is his business."

"Where can I find Dingo?"

Shrug.

"What's Dingo's real name?"

"Pussy!" Mayjack yelled at the ring, where the one slugger was still down, and the fat man was now bending over him. "Get up, Frankie. Get him up, honey boy, get that pussy on his feet."

Hopeless. I could stand here and hammer the same questions for an hour and I'd get nothing more out of Mayjack's scrambled head than what he'd been programmed to deliver.

At that I could count myself lucky. Jackie Spoons didn't consider me a threat; if he had he'd have sent a hardcase or two to deliver the message, with fists and weapons to back it up. Or brought it to me in person. The fact that he'd given the job to a punchdrunk old man was a show of contempt for me and my troubles.

Well, I could live with that—for now. The puzzler was why he'd thrown me Dingo. What was the connection between the two of them, the reason for Jackie Spoons' dislike of the Aussie? And the main question: Was Dingo the bald man? I didn't remember any sort of accent, but Baldy had spoken only a few words, and I'd been under enormous tension; and an Australian might have been in this country long enough to have Americanized his speech. Dingo could be the bald man, all right. Or a link to him. Or nothing more than just another bottom-feeding pawn.

In the car I tried calling Tamara; the line hummed and buzzed emptily. I accessed the office answering machine and listened to three different voices, none of them hers or Nick Kinsella's. No calls, no messages: no news.

Working Sunday for me but not for most other people. Joe DeFalco wasn't home, either.

I couldn't think of anybody else to call, anyplace to go, anybody to see. Tomorrow, yes, but tomorrow was a long way off. I drove around for a while, aimlessly; all it did was give me too much down time to spin my thoughts and listen to the clicks. So I went home to Kerry and Emily and took them to the Palace of Fine Arts and then the aquarium and then to North Beach for an Italian dinner. Keeping them close, surrounding our little unit with strangers— getting through the rest of the day.

But none of it was much good. Nothing was going to be much good until I found Baldy. Only then would I be able to start living again.

14

BEN DURYEA HAD ONE OF THE MORE thankless jobs in law enforcement. For nearly a quarter of a century he'd been a parole agent for the California Department of Corrections. Parole agents are what they're called now, to distinguish them from the county-hired probation officers, but oldtimers in or close to the system still refer to the breed as either parole officers or POs.

The thing about POs is that they work like dogs. Each has a caseload that is supposed to run around one hundred, but because of prison overcrowding and little enough funding to increase a too-low workforce of some eighteen hundred agents, most carried between a hundred-and-fifty and two hundred cases. Their job was to provide general supervision of criminal offenders and to help them adjust to life in the community after their release, which in fact meant arranging jobs, housing, medical care, counseling, education, social activities; traveling widely to interview clients, family members, acquaintances, employers; conducting searches, surveillance, and drug testing when necessary; and making arrests of parole violators, agents being required by law to carry firearms. For all of which duties they were paid between forty thousand and fifty thousand dollars, annually, before taxes. The attrition rate was pretty high; only dedication, inertia, and decent civil service benefits kept it from being much higher.

I caught Duryea in his office at the Ferry Building early Monday morning—just barely. He was getting ready to leave on a three-day trip to the Salinas-Monterey area, where half a dozen of his clients were currently located. POs spend a lot of time away from their desks and on the road. I was fortunate to connect with him at all without an appointment.

"I can give you ten minutes," he said. "What do you need?"

"A line on one of your people. He may have information connected to a case I'm working."

"Something I should know about?"

"I can't be sure until I talk to him."

"You'll let me know if there is?"

"Right away."

"What's his name?"

"Charlie Bright. Charles Andrew Bright."

"Bright, Bright. I don't . . . wait a minute." He leaned over to flick on his computer, then tapped the keyboard and squinted at the screen through black-rimmed glasses. He looked tired, the kind of weariness that makes an intaglio of a man's face. I had a dim memory of Duryea as a young PO with a fresh degree in criminology from Cal State Fullerton, lean and earnest and full of zeal. Now he was twenty pounds heavier, yet he still seemed almost gaunt; the lines in his forehead and cheeks were deep-cut, and his once prominent widow's peak had thinned and receded at least three inches. It takes a toll, all right. His kind of work—and mine.

"Oh, yeah, Charles Andrew Bright." Duryea took off his glasses briefly to rub his eyes. "There was a time," he said ruefully, "when I prided myself on instant recall—all my clients' names, addresses, phone numbers, personal data. Now I can barely remember to take a leak when I get up in the morning."

"I hear you."

"Bright's low-priority, though. You know his history?"

"Some of it."

"No problems since he was released. Regular reports. What do you want to know?"

"For starters, what he looks like. I've never seen him."

"Skinny kid. Red hair, blue eyes, freckles."

Scratch Charlie Bright. "What's his current address?"

"Let's see . . . rooming house in Oakland."

"Employed where?"

"Warehouseman and driver for Eastside Meat Packers in Emeryville."

He gave me both addresses, and I wrote them down. "How about relatives in the area?" I asked then.

"No relatives in California. One aunt in Texas, but she's in a nursing home."

"Other contacts?"

"Not as far as I know. He keeps pretty much to himself these days, or so he claims."

I asked, "Any of these names in his files?" and ticked off Dingo, Jay Cohalan, and Jackie Spoons. Negative on each. If there was a connection between Bright and any of them, it was buried.

"Anything else?" Duryea said.

"Well, I can use a copy of Bright's photo."

"That's against the rules."

"I know it. But technically so is giving out verbal information to somebody not in the system. Just a small extension of the favor, Ben."

He made a blowing sound. The young Ben Duryea might have refused me; the tired, middle-aged Ben Duryea said, "I suppose if I had my printer on and I happened to hit the right buttons and you happened to be standing over here while my back was turned. . . ."

He tapped a couple of keys and the printer began to hum and whir. It didn't take long for a photo printout to appear. Duryea was on his feet, shrugging into his jacket, when I plucked Charlie

Bright's likeness out of the tray, glanced at it briefly, and folded it into my pocket.

"Time for me to hit the road," he said. He straightened his tie, yawned, rotated his head the way you do when your neck is stiff, and then grimaced. "Christ, some days. I'm getting too old for this job."

"Some jobs are like that."

"Don't tell me you never think about packing it in, spending more time with your family instead of with the bottom feeders. Hell, your face looks like you got into it with one or two of that type recently."

He'd been too busy to read the papers or listen to TV news, which allowed me to ignore the second statement and respond only to the first. "Sometimes," I said.

"I think about it a lot. But I probably won't do it. Die on the job instead of in the saddle at home in bed . . . of a massive coronary if not some jerkoff's Saturday night special. My problem is, I never learned how to relax. Maybe guys like us can learn, though. You think?"

"Maybe," I said. "Maybe we can."

I drove across the Bay Bridge to Emeryville and Eastside Meat Packers. The burly warehouse foreman I spoke to there pulled a disgusted face when I asked for Charlie Bright. "Not working today," he said. "Called in sick again."

"Again?"

"Getting to be a habit the past few weeks. We don't mind giving ex-cons a break, but they got to show up regular and pull their weight. Bright's not doing either one. I told him this morning—one more sick day and his ass is fired."

The rooming house address Ben Duryea had given me was in a semi-industrial area close to downtown Oakland. The woman who ran the place said, "He don't live here anymore. I kicked him out more than two weeks ago."

"Why?"

"Didn't pay his rent, that's why. I don't allow freeloaders. Pay up on time or they're history."

"Why didn't you report this to his parole officer? Isn't that what you're supposed to do?

"Told my daughter to take care of that. Mean she didn't? Damn that girl; I can't trust her to do nothing except run around with that no-good boyfriend of hers."

I checked back with Eastside Meat Packers by phone, used Ben Duryea's name to get their personnel department to look up Bright's employee file. The address they had for him was the Oakland rooming house. Bright hadn't bothered to inform his employers that he'd moved, either.

When I walked into the office shortly before noon, Tamara said, "You're lucky you got me as your assistant, you know it?"

"Sure I know it. What'd you do that makes you look so smug?"

"Some PR, my man."

"What kind of PR?"

"Media kind, best there is. Reporter and cameraman from Channel Seven showed up a while ago, wanted an interview about the two murders. You know about Cohalan getting wasted, right?"

"Fuentes called me in yesterday to ID the body. Didn't I mention that in my phone message?"

"No, and they done surprised me with it. But I was smooth as silk. Gave 'em their interview and plenty more."

"Tamara . . . what'd you tell them?"

"Nothing you won't like, don't worry. What a fine detective you are, how you always putting out for our clients, how much you taught me. No bullshit, just the wide-eyed truth. Man, they ate it up."

"Terrific."

"Yeah," she said, misreading my reaction. "Now I'm glad I let Horace talk me into upscaling my image. I'm gonna look like I belong on Oprah, foxy black lady PI with butter just oozin' out my mouth. We'll have to beat off the new clients with a stick."

Maybe so, but it did not set well with me; I wished she hadn't done it. The last thing I needed right now was more media attention, a rush of new clients. But I didn't say any of this to Tamara. Why burst her bubble? She was pleased with herself, believed she'd done a good thing with the best of intentions. So young, such a child of the new fast-track millenium where image and publicity and self-promotion ruled. Intellectually she understood what had happened to me Friday night, but its emotional baggage and effects were not within her experience. And I hoped to God they never would be. No one can understand what it's like to be a victim of mindless violence except the survivors.

I asked her, "When did they say the interview would air?"

"Tonight. Six o'clock news."

"If I'm near a TV I'll be sure to watch," I lied.

"No problem if you're not. I already called up Horace and told him to tape it."

I eased her off the subject by saying, "Right now we've got work to do. Any new information for me?"

"One piece on Byers. May not mean much."

"Give."

"Girl didn't graduate with her high school class in Lodi. Never did get her diploma. Made me wonder, so I accessed some public records. What do you think?"

"Pregnant?"

"Right on. Knocked up at seventeen."

"She have the baby?"

"Six-pound, nine-ounce boy. Kevin Paul."

"Who's the father?"

"Grant Johnson. Year older, went to the same high school."

"He marry her?"

"Nope. Not in California or Nevada, anyway."

"Who ended up with the kid? Not Byers?"

"Still working on that. Might be the father, might be she gave it up for adoption."

"What else have you got on Grant Johnson?"

"Born in Lodi like Byers, played football and basketball in high school, worked as a truck driver and plumber's helper before and after graduation. No criminal record."

"Family wouldn't be Australian, by any chance?"

"Uh-uh. American WASP."

"See if you can get a photo of him anyway, or at least a general description."

"Will do."

"Here's some more work for you. Pull up whatever you can on a character named Jackie Spoons—strongarm type reputed to be involved in the crystal meth trade. He's a Greek, real name Andropopolous or something similar. What I'm most interested in is a connection between him and Dingo or any other Australian, him and Jay Cohalan and/or Charlie Bright."

"You think one of those dudes is Baldy?"

"Not Jackie Spoons or Bright. But they might be mixed up with him in some way."

Tamara's self-satisfaction had rubbed away. She seemed to be seeing me clearly for the first time since I came in; her brown eyes showed concern. "You look tired," she said. "You okay? I mean. . . ."

"I know what you mean. Hanging in there."

"Truly?"

"Truly."

"That's my dawg," she said, but she wasn't smiling.

I brought a cup of coffee to my desk. Tamara had laid a message on the blotter to call Joe DeFalco at the *Chronicle*. When I got DeFalco on the line, I ran the bunch of names by him. The only one that rang bells was Jay Cohalan, and only because of the double homicide.

"Check your morgue files, will you, Joe? See if you can turn up any links among Jackie Spoons, Dingo, and the others."

"Quid pro quo," he said. "If there's an exclusive here. . . ."

"You'll get it, don't worry. Same deal we've always had."

"That Sentinels business," he said reminiscently. "Man, I should've had a Pulitzer nomination for my expose."

"Your expose. Right. Joe DeFalco, fearless investigative reporter. All you did, buddy, was write up what I handed you."

"Sure, but I wrote it so damn *well*."

Joe DeFalco, egotist and bullshitter.

I had some other casework to do, but my head wasn't into it. I plugged away sporadically while Tamara went to get us a cold lunch; gave it up and considered a call to Nick Kinsella. Counterproductive, I decided. He was not a man you could prod, especially not when he was doing you a favor.

On impulse I took the plastic chip out of my wallet and studied it again, trying to get an idea. I'd shown it to Kerry yesterday, but if it was some kind of advertising gimmick, she knew nothing about it. Thumbing through the Yellow Pages had been a waste of time. Lucky Buffalo Chip. Remember the Alamo! Signifying what, and why had Cohalan been carrying the chip?

I was still fiddling with it when Tamara came back. She plunked one of two paper sacks down in front of me, paused, and then asked, "What's that you got there?"

Young eyes, eagle eyes. I showed her the chip.

"Oh, yeah," she said. "The Alamo."

"You recognize this?"

"Sure. Don't tell me you hang out down there."

"Down where?"

"The Alamo. Somebody gave it to you, huh?"

"Mel Bishop. Carolyn Dain found it in her husband's pocket."

"No shit?"

"Tamara."

"Sorry. Doesn't seem like that dude's scene, either."

"*What* scene? What's the Alamo?"

"Mean you don't know?"

"Would I be asking if I did?"

"Salsa scene. Tex-mex food and music."

"Restaurant? Club?"

"Both. Big place down the Peninsula, tex-mex barbecue on one side, salsa club on the other."

"Where down the Peninsula?"

"Belmont."

Belmont was one of the towns strung like beads between San Francisco and San Jose, a good twenty-five miles south and close to Redwood City, where Tamara's father was on the police force and she'd been born and raised.

"And they give these out to their customers?"

"Right. To anybody spends twenty-five bucks or more. Good for a dollar off in the bar or restaurant. 'Remember the Alamo!' so you won't forget where you got it."

"How recently were you there?"

"Six months, about. Horace likes barbecue, I like to boogie."

"What kind of place is it?"

"Just told you, tex-mex food and salsa music—"

"I don't mean that. What kind of clientele?"

"Young folks, mostly. Cool crowd."

"It have any kind of rep?"

"Rep? Oh, like a drug deli?"

"Like that."

"Not that I've heard."

"But some people who go there use drugs."

"Some people everywhere use drugs."

"My point is, you could score there if you had the right connections."

"Same answer. You can score just about anywhere if you got the right connections. Think that's why Cohalan went to the Alamo?"

"There're tex-mex restaurants and salsa clubs here in the city," I said. "Belmont's a long way from his office downtown, a long way from Daly City."

"Well, could be he didn't like to pick up his pussy . . . 'scuse me, his women too close to home. Could be that's where he met Byers."

"Also possible. But I still like the drug angle." I took the chip from Tamara, returned it to my wallet. "There's something else that makes me like it, too."

She was smiling now, that knowing little grin of hers. Quick on the uptake, as always. "Gotcha," she said. "Charlie Bright."

Born in Texas, and the Alamo was a tex-mex hangout. Arrested with Byers for dealing methamphetamines, and both Byers and Cohalan were crankheads. Somebody had been supplying them. Maybe Jackie Spoons, maybe the Aussie called Dingo . . . and maybe a young guy on parole who had suddenly begun missing work and changed his address without telling his PO, both indicators of drug-related recidivism.

"Yeah," I said. "Charlie Bright."

15

THE ALAMO WAS A BIG HACIENDA-STYLE place, stucco and exposed beams and tile roof, that took up most of a block just off El Camino Real. A neon roof sign spelled out the name in a garish dazzle of pink and green and yellow. All of the exterior was brightly lit. Floodlights trained on the stucco walls showed them to have been painted pink; other floods illuminated a good-sized parking lot that extended from the front around on one side.

The lot was half full when I got there at seven o'clock. I found an empty space about equidistant between the two main entrances, one neon-marked *Restaurant*, the other *Salsa*, and went in through the latter. More bright neon tubing, muraled walls, booths and tables, and a slick-looking dance floor ringing a center bar. At the far end was a dais, empty now except for half a dozen standing microphones; it was too early for live music, if they even had a band performing on Mondays. Canned Latin music blared from loud-speakers. Two large TV sets mounted on opposite walls showed a Monday Night Football game in progress. Most of the twenty or so patrons were watching the game—silent, violent action played out in pantomime to the hammering salsa beat, not my idea of an ideal combination.

I made my way to the bar, scanning faces as I went. Nearly all were young, twenties and thirties, and none was familiar. I ordered a bottle of Dos Equis, in keeping with the motif, and when the black-shirted bartender served it, I showed him the photo printout of Charlie Bright, saying that Bright was the son of an old friend, and I'd been told he was a regular here. The bartender squinted in the dim light, shook his head. "Don't know him, man." I asked if he knew anybody named Dingo. Another headshake and a walkaway.

There was one cocktail waitress on duty; I got the same negative response from her. For twenty minutes I stayed put at the bar, nursing the beer. People came in, people went out. No Charlie Bright. A pair of swing doors had a green-neon *Restaurant* sign over them; I walked over and entered the other half of the Alamo.

Crowded in there, men, women, and kids stuffing themselves in booths and at tables. A young hostess outfitted in a peasant blouse and a flaring Mexican skirt led me to a corner table. Her reaction to the photo was a shrug, a half-smile, and "Sorry, I never seen him before." Mexico by way of Brooklyn or the Bronx.

I hadn't eaten since lunch, so I ordered a small plate of barbecue beef brisket and managed to get most of it down. Too edgy to care much about food. Stranger surrounded by strangers in a strange land, waiting for one familiar face that didn't appear.

Back into the club. More young people now, none of them Bright. A second waitress had come on duty; I took a table in her section. Well, she said when she'd had a look at Bright's likeness, maybe she'd seen him once or twice, but she couldn't be sure. "We get a lot of customers—this is a real popular place, you know?" As for Dingo: "That's a funny name. I don't know anybody with a funny name like that."

I nursed another bottle of Dos Equis. The big room kept filling up, a good crowd for a Monday night. More strangers. And I began to stand out among them: I was more than twice the age of ninety percent of the clientele. Glances, open looks, a few whispered exchanges. I kept glancing at my watch, fidgeting, staring toward the entrance—making it plain that I was waiting for somebody who should have shown up long ago. But I couldn't keep up the pretense indefinitely. And the canned music seemed louder, more strident, and strobe lights had begun flashing over the dance floor. The racket, the assault of colored lights created a surreal atmosphere, impairing my vision and giving me a headache. In that pulsing, light-and-dark crush of bodies I would have had trouble recognizing Kerry from more than a few feet away.

I gave it up, went out into the cold night and walked around until my head cleared. Then I got into the car, rolled the window partway down, and sat there feeling frustrated. After nine now. Long damn day, and nothing much to show for it. No news from Joe DeFalco that I didn't already know, no word from Nick Kinsella, no new leads or additional data on Annette Byers' illegitimate son. And now tonight, no Dingo and no Charlie Bright.

Hang around here how much longer? Couple of hours? Until midnight? I ought to go home, get some sleep. Sure, but I knew I wouldn't sleep much; mostly lie wide-eyed in the dark, listening to Kerry's breathing, listening to the clicks. Might as well stay put, wrapped in the dark cocoon of the car, for as long as I could stand it.

I called the condo to let Kerry know I would be late. We didn't talk long. She was fine, Emily was fine, I was fine—there did not seem to be much else to say long distance.

Minutes died slowly after that. Another stakeout, another handful of lost time. Most of my life spent in situations like this, waiting, vegetating. Suspended animation. Dying by inches and clock ticks.

Better than already being dead, I thought.

Better than lying in cold storage like Carolyn Dain and her husband.

Yes, sure, but they didn't know it. Awareness for them had ceased; time for them stood still. By the grace of God I had been granted more minutes, hours, days, months, maybe years, and here I was killing off some of that precious gift in another dark, lifeless stakeout. Didn't I owe it to myself, to Kerry and Emily, to use what time I had left in healthier, pleasanter ways?

Kerry's voice echoed in my mind. *You can't keep on doing the things you did twenty or thirty years ago.... The hunter, always the hunter.... Can't you understand I need you, Emily needs you—alive safe?*

And Ben Duryea's. *Christ, some days. I'm getting too old for this job.... My problem is, I never learned how to relax. Maybe guys like us can learn, though.*

And mine to Duryea: *Maybe we can.* And mine to Kerry: *Maybe you're right.*

Maybe, maybe, maybe. . . .

Ten o'clock. Cars rolled into the lot, faces appeared and then disappeared inside the Alamo. A parade of unknowns. A wasteland of strangers.

Ten-thirty.

Ten-forty.

And another car entered the lot, this one moving a little too fast so that its tires squealed on the turn and when the driver braked on the blacktop. I watched its lights swing away from where I was, loop around to the side, and then come back again. Looking for a parking space, finally finding one in the row behind me. The driver hopped out, passed alone between two cars twenty yards to my left—into the garish light from the neon and one of the floodlights.

Charlie Bright.

Tall, thin, red-haired, wearing a Western-style shirt and Levi's and sharp-toed cowboy boots. Unmistakably Charlie Bright.

He was in a hurry, almost running. Man with a purpose, heading straight for the club entrance. Briefly I thought about going in after him, but it would have been a mistake; too many people in there, too much chance of him either making trouble or disappearing on me. Wiser to wait out here, brace him when he returned to his car . . . no matter how long it took.

Didn't take long at all, as it turned out. Less than ten minutes. And there he was coming through the club entrance, still in a hurry, moving on a line toward where his car was parked. But I didn't get out and brace him as I'd planned because he was no longer alone.

The guy with him had a fireplug build, wore a black hat and a fringed suede jacket. He moved at an almost leisurely pace, forcing Bright to lag back to keep from outdistancing him. When they passed parallel to me, I heard Bright say in an agitated Texas drawl, "Come on, man, let's don't take all night," and the fireplug answer, "Stay loose, will you," and Bright again, fading, " . . . told you, I got to have. . . ."

I adjusted the rearview mirror, couldn't see them, and put the window down and fiddled with the side mirror until I picked them up in the shadows alongside Bright's wheels. Two blobs doing something that I couldn't make out, but it did not take much imagination to figure what it was. Drug deal, money and methamphetamines or some other controlled substance changing hands. From the snatch of dialogue I'd overheard, it seemed Bright was the buyer.

I started the engine, put on the lights, crawled out of the space and around toward the street exit. From the edge of the row where Bright was parked I could see that the two of them had finished their transaction; the fireplug was backtracking to the club and Bright was getting into his car. I stayed put, idling, a wait of no more than five seconds. He fast-backed out of the space, came flying past me and aimed for El Camino when he cleared the lot.

The red light there slowed him up, gave me time to roll close behind and get a good look at what he was driving. Ford Taurus, light-colored, newish. The license plate was dirt-smeared, and in the uncertain light I couldn't tell if one of the numerals was a three or an eight. The light changed; he was off again, not quite jumping it, into a left on El Camino.

I repeated the Ford's plate number aloud half a dozen times, committing it to memory with both a three and an eight in sequence. Half a mile north, another red light caught Bright, but an SUV slid in behind him before I could get there. I drew up alongside him, going slow. The angle was wrong for a clear reading of the Ford's plate.

He led me straight up El Camino through San Carlos. Still driving fast, but not recklessly—not with drugs in the car. Red light again at the San Mateo line; I couldn't maneuver in behind him there, either. I hung back in his lane this time: changing lanes and speeds is an effective way to keep a subject from spotting a tail.

A few streets beyond the Hillsdale Shopping Center, Bright made a sudden sharp left turn without either slowing or signaling. The move caught me fifty yards back; and I had to wait for a couple of sets of oncoming headlights to clear before I could swing after him. He was two blocks away by then. As I accelerated, the Ford's taillights flashed and he went sliding around another corner, pointing north once more.

When I got there and started my turn I saw him again—making an illegal U-turn in the middle of the street. My first thought was that he'd spotted me after all, was going to try some crazy stunt to elude me or force a confrontation. But that wasn't it. A parking place was what he was after, in front of a four-story apartment complex that took up the entire east side of the block.

Along the west side was a solid line of parked cars; there was nothing I could do but keep on going, past where Bright was now jockeying the Ford into the space—the only damn space on the entire block. I had to go all the way to the next corner before I could pull off, and at that I had to park illegally in front of a fire hydrant.

On foot I cut across the street, not quite running. When I came onto the sidewalk I could see Bright leave the Ford, head up the front walk to the apartment building's main entrance. Seconds later he was gone inside. By the time I got there, there was no sign of him in the lighted lobby.

The banks of aluminum mailboxes lining both vestibule walls totaled twenty-four on each—forty-eight apartments. All but two of the name slots were filled, and none of the names was Bright. Living in one of the unmarked apartments, or living here under another name, or visiting one of the tenants, or holed up with one of the tenants. And I had no good way of immediately finding out which. You can't start ringing door buzzers at eleven o'clock at night and expect to get cooperative responses.

I went back down to the curb and found the Ford Taurus. The street was empty; I tried both doors. Locked. Naturally. Even screwed-up parole violators locked their cars nowadays. At the rear I squatted to check the license plate. The one numeral in question was an eight.

Bright's car? Or somebody else's that he'd borrowed? Unless I wanted to hang around for another, almost certainly futile stakeout, I'd have to wait until tomorrow for the answer. And to find out what, if anything, Charlie Bright knew about the bald man.

Tomorrow was soon enough, I decided. I'd waited this long; I could wait a few hours longer.

A Department of Motor Vehicles check used to be a simple proposition. The names and addresses of California's registered vehicle owners were a matter of public record and could be accessed by anyone. That all changed some years ago when a TV actress was murdered by a stalker who'd gotten her address through the DMV. The new antistalking laws, which included the sealing of DMV records to the general public, are necessary and laudable, and I wouldn't have them any other way, but they do make my job more difficult. Even with Tamara and her computer skills and a cultivated DMV contact, it takes a while for a detective agency to get a plate number run and the particulars on its owner.

I sat in the office, fidgeting, waiting for Tamara to lay the necessary groundwork. It was one of those cold, gray, bleak mornings that give vent to indecision and self-doubt. The fact that I was tired and headachey after a dream-plagued night didn't help matters any. I kept wondering if I'd have been better off going straight to San Mateo and staking out the apartment complex and the Ford Taurus; calling Tamara for the DMV check instead of coming here to the office. What if Bright was gone when I finally did get there? What if the name of the Ford's owner didn't match any of the building's tenants? What if, what if.

I called Eastside Meat Packers, to find out if Bright had gone to work today. Negative. This time he hadn't even bothered to call in and it had cost him his job. So if what I'd witnessed last night was in fact a drug buy, it could be that Bright was too stoned or strung out today to drive to Emeryville, which in turn made it likely that he was still somewhere in that San Mateo apartment complex. The thought made me feel a little more positive.

As I watched Tamara at her Mac computer, it occurred to me that if I wasn't so damn stubborn and technophobic and rooted in the old ways, and had learned computer skills myself long ago, I could run DMV checks myself instead of having to rely on her all the time. I could be sitting down there in San Mateo with a laptop doing two things at once, not killing time but making good use of it. Too late for this old dog to learn new tricks? Probably, given my disposition and temperament. The world wasn't mine any longer; it belonged to Tamara and her generation. And that included the detective business . . . her business now as much as mine. Why not step aside then, let her take it all the way into the twenty-first century? She was fully capable of making it grow and prosper in the new millenium as I never could.

I was brooding on that when she said, "Got it. Want me to print it out for you?"

"No. Just read it off."

"Ford's registered to Kirsten Sabat, S-a-b-a-t, nineteen-o-nine Third Avenue, San Mateo."

Nineteen-o-nine Third Avenue was the address of the apartment complex. I worked my memory, but I couldn't recall if Kirsten Sabat had been one of the names on the mailboxes. Too many names, too late at night, and I'd been too focused on Charlie Bright.

Tamara asked, "Want me to run a driver's license and employment check on her?"

"Might as well." I was already on my feet, shrugging into my overcoat. "But it's low prority. Dingo, Jackie Spoons, Annette Byers' background first."

"Right. I should have something pretty soon on the father of her bastard kid. You going to San Mateo?'

I nodded. "Keep me updated."

"You do the same, hear?"

Tamara called sooner than expected, and not for the reason she'd indicated. I was still in the city, just climbing the entrance ramp to 101 South near the city's best new construction in years, Pac Bell Park, when the car phone buzzed.

She said, "Man just called for you. Nick Kinsella."

"About time. What'd he say?"

"Wants to see you. Said he's got something for you."

"Tell you what it is?"

"Wouldn't say."

"Where is he? Blacklight Tavern?"

"Yup."

"Change of plans then," I said. "The Blacklight and Kinsella first, then San Mateo."

16

"MAN, YOU'RE IN SOME BIG HURRY," KINSELLA said. "I figure it can't be more than ten minutes since I talked to the girl in your office. What'd you do, fly over here?"

"I was in the neighborhood. What've you got for me, Nick?"

"Dingo, that's what I got."

"What about Dingo?"

He made his chair creak and groan, leaning back. His desk was strewn with more food remains—Chinese takeout, probably from the previous night—and the butts and ashes from a couple of dozen dead black stogies. The air in his office was dead, too, murdered by tobacco smoke laden with carcinogens. We were the only two people in there trying to breathe it this morning.

He tore the wrapper off another stogie, bit off one crooked end, fired it with a gold-and-platinum lighter. Taking his time, enjoying himself. That was Kinsella: fat, sloppy, corrupt, with a flair for the dramatic and a vicious streak on the one hand, a tempering one of generosity toward people he liked on the other. I didn't prod him. When you dealt with Kinsella, you played down on his level, according to his rules, or you didn't play at all.

"Ah," he said when he had the stogie drawing to his satisfaction. "Nothing like a good cigar. 'A woman's just a woman, but a good cigar's a smoke.' Who was it said that?"

"I'm not sure. Kipling, maybe."

"Who's Kipling?"

"Long-dead British writer."

"Yeah, a limey. Figures." He made the chair creak and groan again. "So like I said, Dingo."

I waited.

"I figure maybe he's your shooter," Kinsella said.

I could feel myself go tight, inside and out, all at once. "Bald? Bushy eyebrows? In his forties?"

"So I hear."

"Who is he?"

"Nobody much. One of these shit-for-brains guys, apes walking around on two legs. Like Bluto, you remember Bluto from the other night? Big guys, tough, but zombies from the neck up."

"What's his real name?"

"That I don't have. Nobody seems to know."

"His connection to Jackie Spoons?"

"Word is he worked for Jackie awhile," Kinsella said, "about a year ago. They had some hassle over money—Jackie figured Dingo screwed up on a collection, tried to hold out a little for himself. Beat the crap out of him, busted his leg. What I told you, he's crazy. Jackie, I mean."

"Where can I find Dingo?"

"You figure I'm right, he's the guy almost put you in a pine box?"

I said between my teeth, "I'll know that when I see him."

"You figure on putting *him* in a pine box?"

"Where, Nick?"

"Beats me. Beats everybody I talked to."

"Who knows him besides Jackie?"

"Nobody knows him, me included. He's what you call your mystery man."

"Maybe Jackie knows where he is."

"Uh-uh. He ain't had nothing to do with Dingo since the hassle; he can't help you. Stay away from him, you know what's good for you. That's from him as well as me."

"Is Dingo a crankhead?"

"What you think? He worked for Jackie, even Jackie uses what he peddles." Kinsella shook his head. "Drugs, they're for the apes and the schmucks and the losers. You got to keep a clear head, you want to climb up on top and stay there. No drugs, no booze. No broads, either, except once in a while. Just a lot of good cigars."

"Anything else you can tell me?"

He shrugged, blew smoke at me, shrugged again. "You got your favor, my friend," he said. "You got all I got. Like they say, now the ball's in your court."

The Ford Taurus was no longer parked in front of the San Mateo apartment complex. Nor anywhere else in the vicinity; I drove around two full blocks to make sure the car hadn't been moved to another spot.

It bothered me a little, but not as much as it would have before I talked to Kinsella. I found a place to put my car and went to have another look at the mailboxes in the building's vestibule. Kirsten Sabat—Apt. 411. That was something, anyway.

I was about to ring the bell when two young women wearing flight attendants' outfits and dragging wheeled suitcases emerged from the elevator inside. San Francisco International was not that far from here; a lot of the apartments were probably occupied by airline personnel. These two were in a hurry. They came out through the entrance doors without a glance my way or a backward look as they clattered down the steps. Sometimes problems get solved before they develop, and this was one of them. I caught the door before it shut and slipped inside with the same straight-ahead purpose, as if I belonged there as much as the stewardesses.

The elevator deposited me on the fourth floor. Number 411 was an inside unit, no doubt facing on an inner courtyard: the complex was built in a massive enclosed rectangle. There was a bell push and one of those one-way magnifying peepholes; I laid my thumb on the button, kept it there for three or four seconds with my face arranged into a hopeful salesman's smile. I needn't have bothered. That ring and two others brought no response.

The door had two locks—push-button snap variety on the knob, a deadbolt above. I rotated the knob, pushed and pulled just enough to tell that the deadbolt was off. Another problem solved in embryo. Snap locks are an open invitation; a preteen can loid one with a little knowledge and a little patience. I got out a credit card, made sure I had the hall to myself, and went to work. It took about four minutes to get the plastic positioned just right to snick the bolt free. Just like on TV, only not as fast.

The apartment was a mess. At first glance it appeared to have been ransacked, but sunlight streaming in through the open drapes showed me that the clutter was cumulative—a slob's paradise of male and female clothing, disarranged furniture, dirty dishes, over-flowing ashtrays, and general disorder. The acrid scent of mari-juana flavored the air; half the butts in the one ashtray I glanced at were dead roaches. There was also what looked to be a rock of methamphetamine, at least two grams. Charlie Bright and Kirstan Sabat: soulmates.

I made my way through the obstacle course to have a look at the other rooms. The kitchen invited ants, rodents, and a case of disin-fectant. A short hallway gave access to a bathroom on one side, a bedroom on the other. The bedroom door was open; I started in there. And pulled up short one pace across the threshhold.

Somebody was lying facedown on the bed.

Covers pulled up to the neck, male, red hair—Charlie Bright.

The last person I'd come across lying facedown on a bed had been Carolyn Dain. That thought and Bright's stillness built cold tension in me as I advanced to the bed. I caught an edge of the stained blanket, drew it down halfway, and then let breath hiss out between my teeth. Bright was alive, unhurt. Sound asleep. Up close, I could hear the kind of wheezing that comes from clogged sinuses.

I dug fingers into his shoulder and shook him. Did it twice more, hard and rough. It was like shaking a rubber dummy; the only response I got was a couple of faint grunts. I gripped his other shoulder and flopped him over on his back. No response to that, either. The red hair was long and tangled, his skin grub white where it wasn't spotted with freckles, and he was thinner than he'd looked in the photo, almost anorexic. You could see each of his ribs, the shape of his breastbone above a concave belly. He couldn't have weighed more than 120, even though he was nearly six feet tall.

I slapped his face half a dozen times, back and forth, not being gentle about it. All that got me was a low groan. Another set of six slaps, and his eyes popped open; but there was no focus in them, and they closed again before I finished smacking him. The hell with this, I thought. I don't like mishandling the helpless, even a kid who probably deserved it.

So I yanked the covers all the way off his naked body, hauled him off the bed and onto his feet. It roused him enough to mutter something that sounded like "What's going on?" but not enough to enable him to walk under his own power. I had to drag him out of there and across the hall into the bathroom. There was a shower stall; I pushed him in there, propped him against a mildewed tile wall, and turned on the cold water.

That brought him out of it. He squealed when the spray hit him; gasped, moaned, made other sounds of protest. But he took it standing up and without trying to get away. I figured he'd had enough when his eyes stayed open and shivers wracked him. I turned off the water, tossed him one of the soiled towels draped over a clothes hamper.

From the hallway I watched him dry off in jerky movements, wrap the towel around his middle. He stood for a few seconds, staring groggily at nothing. Then he gulped three glasses of water, dribbling some of it down his skinny chest, and wobbled past me into the bedroom. He sat on the edge of the bed, put his face in his hands.

I leaned against a bureau, waiting. His head came up finally. The watery blue eyes had focus now; he saw me standing there and gave me a long, bleary look. He didn't seem angry or scared—just bewildered in a fuzzy-headed way, and maybe a little resigned. As if it were an expected part of his lot to be hauled out of bed and thrown in the shower by somebody he'd never seen before. The mildmannered, submissive variety of addict and ex-con. Yet another variety of bleeder. The predatory cons in prison must have had a field day with him.

"Who're you?" he asked. The Texas drawl had a mush-mouthed sound, as though his tongue was swollen.

"A man with questions. A man you don't want to lie to or mess with."

"Cop?"

"Close enough. Your PO's a good friend of mine."

"Mr. Duryea? Oh, shit." Some scare had come into his voice. "He know I'm here?"

"Not yet. Cooperate and he won't find out from me."

"Gonna find out anyways, sure as hell. Goddamn that Kay. I wished I never met her."

"Who's Kay?"

"Kirsten. I was clean till I met her. Clean and straight, I swear it. I'd've known all the shit she was into, I never would've come near her. Speed, man, that stuff messes with your head. I feel like I done crashed and burned."

"She didn't knock you down and force you to take it, did she?"

"Well, she had it, she offered it, she's got good connections. . . ." He grimaced, groaned a little. "Ah, hell, it ain't her fault. It's mine. I know better, I just cain't hep myself sometimes. Man don't use his head, he might's well have two assholes."

Amen to that.

Bright looked around the bedroom, frowning. "She ain't here, is she?"

"Just the two of us."

"What time's it?"

"After eleven."

"Eleven? Goddamn her, she knows I cain't wake up like she does after a jag. I told her get me up so's I can go to work. No later'n eight A.M. and don't forget 'cause I cain't take no more time off."

"Maybe she tried to get you up. Look at the trouble I had three hours later."

"Yessir, I'm sorry about that. But listen here, I got to call in. I lose that job of mine, Mr. Duryea's gonna violate my ass for sure."

There was no point in telling him he'd already lost his job. "Answer my questions first. A few more minutes won't make any difference."

"Reckon you got that right."

"Dingo," I said.

"Huh?"

"Dingo. You know the name."

"Nossir, I . . . whoa. You mean that Aussie sumbitch?"

"That's right."

"Oh, man, I wished I never set eyes on that boy. I doan want nothing more to do with him."

"What's his real name?"

"I doan know."

"He never told you, you never heard it?"

"Nossir. Dingo's all I know."

"Let's make sure we're talking about the same man. Forty or so, big, bald, bushy eyebrows, onion breath."

"Cain't say about his breath. Rest of it's right."

"He speak with an Australian accent?"

"Not so's you notice. Been in this country awhile, I reckon."

Or born here. "All right. Where'd you meet him?"

"Frisco. 'Bout two years back."

"Before you were busted for dealing meth."

"Yessir. All his idea and his fault, that deal. Him and that woman of his."

"Annette Byers?"

"I doan recall her name."

"Tall, leggy, streaky blond hair, early twenties."

"Big tits? Yeah, that's her. Sumbitch Dingo set us up with a undercover narc and her and me got busted. Not him. He got off clean, that boy."

"Why didn't you take him down with you?"

"I sure wanted to, but she said we dasn't, he'd kill us if we did. He would've, too. Sumbitch's meaner'n a sore-dick dog."

"You have any contact with him since you were paroled?"

"Nossir. No way. I ever see him again, I run the other way."

"How about with the woman?"

"Her neither."

"How'd you get involved with the two of them?"

"Met her one night at this here club in Belmont."

"The Alamo?"

"Right, the Alamo."

"She hang out there or what?"

"Not her, me. She come in one night with some friends."

"Dingo one of them?"

"No. Wasn't 'til later that I met up with him."

"Where was that?"

"Party at some old boy's house."

"What old boy?"

"Slick named . . . Duke. Yeah, Duke."

"Duke what?"

"I doan remember. Honest."

"Where was the house?"

"Frisco somewheres."

"What street?"

"I doan remember."

"What part of the city?"

"I doan know Frisco, man."

"Who else was at this party? Jay Cohalan?"

"Who?"

"Jay Cohalan. Another friend of Annette Byers."

"Never heard the name."

I described Cohalan. Bright said, shaking his head, "Nosir, uh-uh." It sounded like the truth, which made me wrong about him being Cohalan's supplier. It had to have been Dingo, then, through Byers. She was the Alamo connection, not Bright. Cohalan had either met her there as Bright had or she'd taken him there after they were together.

I said, "So Dingo was at this Duke's party. Who invited you? Byers?"

"Yessir. Made it seem like we was gonna ball, her and me, but once we got there she was all over him like a blowfly on a turd. Sweet little piece like her, and him with a face that'd pucker a hog's ass. He must have some whang on him, on'y thing I can figure."

"How'd they hook you into the meth deal?"

"Well, he had some crystal on him and I done bought me some. I was flush at the time, I ain't sayin' how come. Dingo, he says he needed more cash for a big buy he was setting up. I wished I didn't listen to him, but he was pretty slick. Snot-on-a-doorknob slick, that boy. A thousand buy-in gets me a fast five thou on the street. Uh-uh. All that thousand got me was a year in jail."

"Anybody else in on the deal with you three?"

"Nossir. Just us."

"Where was Dingo living then, do you know?"

"With her, I reckon. Couple times we met, it was at her place."

"He have a job? The legit kind, I mean."

"A job . . ." Bright frowned, winced, held his head. "Seems one of 'em said something once 'bout him working part-time for some moving company."

"Which moving company?"

"Doan remember if they said which one."

"But it was in the city?"

"Frisco, yeah, I think it was."

"What else can you tell me about Dingo? Where he came from, other people he knew?"

"Nothing. If I ever knew something else, I done forgot it." He blinked at me again. "That sumbitch in trouble? That how come you asking all these questions?"

"He's in trouble, all right. You don't want to know any more than that."

"Reckon I don't," Bright said. "Can I make my call now? I'm scared as hell I'm gonna lose my job."

"Where'll you be if I need to talk to you again?"

"Huh? Right here, that's where."

"Not moving out on Kirsten?"

"I cain't. I give up my own place on account of her and her goddamn speed. I ain't got nowheres else to go." He turned his hands palms upward, a gesture at once rueful and resigned. "No damn place to go except straight back to jail."

17

So now I had most of it.

Dingo: Second-generation Australian, or else in this country long enough to have lost most of his accent. Possibly a part-time worker for a San Francisco moving company as of two years ago. Crankhead and small-time crank dealer. Shacked up or at least sleeping with Annette Byers before she took up with Jay Cohalan, and evidently still tight with her during the affair. Big, hard, mean, violent, and not very bright—a deadly combination.

Scenario: Cohalan meets Byers, probably at the Alamo. He's already worked out the scam to get his hands on his wife's inheritance in small bites, and makes the mistake of confiding this to Byers. She in turn tells Dingo and the two of them cook up a scheme to doublecross Cohalan and steal Carolyn Dain's money for themselves. She works on Cohalan to go for the big bite, all the remaining inheritance money in one payoff, no doubt using sex as the lure. He gives in, they set it up. And that's when I come into it, the monkey wrench that fouls up the works.

It was Dingo, not Cohalan, that she was waiting for at her apartment Thursday night. Cohalan wasn't supposed to show at all, at least not until it was too late and Dingo and Byers had made off with the cash; that was why she was surprised to see him. And when Dingo finally arrives and finds Cohalan there and the money gone with me, he's furious. Cohalan is the first target of his rage, right away or after he's driven out to Daly City and found Carolyn Dain gone. By this time the money's an obsession fueled by frenzy and drugs. One option is to go after me, but for all he knows I've already turned over the seventy-five thousand. He decides to wait for Carolyn Dain to come home. Meanwhile, sometime that night, they load a beaten-up Cohalan into his car and take him out by Candlestick, one of them driving the Camry and the other following. Exit Cohalan.

When Carolyn Dain returns to her house on Friday, Dingo is waiting for her. She tells him I still have the cash, he forces her to make those calls to my office. Then he kills her and waits for me to make the delivery. He's worked up a pretty good hate for me by then, for all the trouble I've caused him, so I'm scheduled to die, too. After the misfire, the fight, the money grab, he'd still want me dead but not badly enough to risk stalking me. The money's all he really cares about. So he and Byers go on the run, or to ground somewhere, or buy a load of crank to sell, or do any number of other things with the cash.

The scenario played out. That was the way it had gone down, or close to it.

All right. There was one more thing I needed to know, and one thing left for me to do. Yeah, just two little things.

Find out Dingo's real name.

And then find him and Byers.

Tamara was on the phone when I came into the office. So I went and got the San Francisco Yellow Pages and spread them open on my desk. Movers and Full Service Storage. Christ, there were twenty-six pages of listings—full-page ads, half-page ads, spot ads, box ads, and single lines of names and addresses. A couple of hundred companies large and small, from AA Worldwide Moving to Zandor Transportation, Inc. It would take Tamara and me the rest of today and part of tomorrow to canvass all the numbers, and at that we'd get answering machines, nonresponses, and a bunch of uncooperative individuals. . . .

Something tickled the back of my mind, but it got lost when I heard the phone go down on Tamara's desk. I glanced over there. "Anything?"

"Might be," she said. "That was Grant Johnson I was talking to."

"Who?"

"Father of Byers' kid. I finally tracked him down. He's a plumber, lives up in Woodland now."

"And?"

"Married, three kids—two of 'em with the present wife. Third's the boy he had with Byers. So I called him up at work, said I was a reporter for the *Chronicle* and had he seen Byers recently and did he have any idea where she might be."

"Took a chance doing that. What'd he say?"

"Got real upset. Knew she was wanted by the law, but what'd that have to do with him? Said he hadn't seen the bitch in years, didn't want nothing to do with her, don't call him again or he'd sic his lawyer on me and the paper both. Sounded scared to me."

"You think he might've been lying?"

"Hiding something, maybe. Hard to be sure over the phone, you know what I'm saying?"

"Worth talking to in person?"

"Might be, but Woodland's a long way from here."

"Only a couple of hours. What else did you pick up on him?"

"Not much. Your model citizens, him and his wife both. Melanie's her name. No criminal records, one speeding ticket for him five years ago. Belong to the Methodist Church, the PTA, Greenpeace."

"If he's that clean," I mused aloud, "what was he doing with a screwed-up crankhead like Byers?"

"Maybe she wasn't into drugs when he knew her. And you know what they say about a hard-on."

"Yes, and I don't want to hear you say it. What's Johnson's home address in Woodland?"

She consulted her computer screen. "Seven-ninety Rio Oso. Work address: RiteClean Plumbing and Heating, twenty-six hundred Benson Avenue. Also Woodland."

I wrote down the addresses. While I was doing that, the phone rang again. Tamara answered, listened, indicated with her hand that the call was for her.

The Yellow Pages were still spread open on my desk blotter. As I pocketed my notebook, one of the large ads caught and held my eye—and the tickling sensation returned. The ad itself had nothing to do with it. Something else. . . .

Got it. Quickly I flipped pages. There were only three listings under the letter V: Valley Relocation and Storage, Vector Transportation, and Viselli Van and Storage. I smacked my fist down on the page.

Dingo 4.15 V.V.S.

V.V.S.—Viselli Van and Storage.

It was a medium-size place, three stories and truck yard that covered half a block at the foot of Potrero Hill. Dot-com firms had gobbled up some real estate in the area, but the pocket here was still blue-collar industrial by day, a meeting ground for hookers and their johns at night. Business at Viselli Van and Storage must be pretty good; they had an office staff of half a dozen. The one I talked to was a Mrs. Lupinski, a pinch-faced woman in her fifties with gray hair so stiff-looking it might have been lacquered and gold-framed eyeglasses dangling from a silver chain.

"I'm looking for a man who might be employed here," I told her. "An Australian who goes by the nickname Dingo."

The name was like a squirt of lemon juice: her mouth puckered with instant distaste. "What do you want with him?"

"He does work here then?"

"He did until last week, and I don't mind telling you I'm glad he's gone."

"When last week?"

"Thursday."

"Quit or fired?"

"Fired, and rightly so. He started a fight with one of our customers. A fistfight, no less, without any provocation. Are you with the police?"

"Not exactly. Why do you ask?"

"Drugs," she said, lowering her voice. The pucker grew even more pronounced. "He's a drug addict. Did you know that?"

"Yes, ma'am." On drugs, probably, and already out of control when he started the fistfight. It hadn't been much of a step from that to crossing the line into cold-blooded murder. "What's his real name?"

"His name?"

"I know him only as Dingo."

"Manganaris," she said as if it were a dirty word. "Harold Manganaris. Harold is a perfectly good name, but he hated it. He insisted everyone call him by that silly Dingo."

All right. Harold Manganaris. All right.

"Would you spell the last name, please."

She spelled it. "He has a foul mouth, too," she said. "You should have heard some of the things he said to me, to other women here. He should've been fired long ago. *Long* ago."

"Would it be possible for me to see his personnel file?"

"Oh, no, that isn't allowed."

"Well, could you at least give me his home address? And the names and addresses of any relatives? Please, Mrs. Lupinski. It's very important."

She glanced around as though she were afraid someone might be eavesdropping. Then she said conspiratorially, "Just a minute," and went away to her desk for a little time. When she came back she half-whispered a street and apartment number on Duboce.

"Relatives, next of kin?"

"None. He provided only the barest facts. He shouldn't have been hired in the first place, if you ask me."

"Did he have any friends here? Anyone he worked with regularly?"

"No. He's not the kind of man who makes friends. Everyone here disliked him, no one wanted to work closely with him. Even Mr. Viselli disliked him. I can't understand why he wasn't fired long ago."

I thanked her, and she said as I turned to leave, "He belongs in jail. I mean it, that man really should be in jail."

Sooner or later, Mrs. Lupinski.

Sooner or later.

The Duboce address was a rundown apartment hotel a couple of blocks west of Market Street, within hailing distance of the massive and deserted U.S. Mint building—the kind of place that you know as soon as you walk in has rodent, roach, and heating problems. It was also a dead end. I had conversations with a beady-eyed little guy who called himself "the day man," and an elderly tenant who was hanging around the lobby because "I ain't got nothing better to do." They both knew Dingo; they didn't like him any more than Mrs. Lupinski had. He'd lived in the building for close to two years, alone in a single room, and moved out ten months ago. No forwarding address, naturally, since he hadn't bothered to notify Viselli Van and Storage of his change of residence. Kept to himself, hardly spoke to the other tenants—"Snotty son of a bitch when he did say something," the elderly gent volunteered—and seemed not to have spent much time on the premises. Friends: none. Visitors: none that either of them could recall.

You'd think that somebody with an uncommon name like Harold Manganaris would be easy enough to run a background check on, but that's not necessarily the case. Variables, any number of them, make every BG check different. Some take a few hours; others take days, even weeks. There may be an unlimited amount of of data available on what Tamara calls "the information superhighway," but finding it, accessing it, cross-examining it, and fitting it together can be a chore even for a computer hacker with her skills.

I'd called her as soon as I left Viselli Van and Storage, so when I got back to the agency at 3:50 she'd been running Manganaris for about an hour and a half. That was enough time to pull together a workable preliminary package—if the variables were few and favorable. But they weren't. When you want something badly enough, the universe being the perverse place it is, that's often the way things shake out.

Tamara wagged her head and said, "No luck so far. I accessed public and CJIS records and most of the Bay Area phone directories. Nobody named Manganaris listed anywhere, no record of birth or marriage, no county, state or federal criminal record or outstanding warrants. Man's never been arrested, at least in California."

"Lucky until now. What about the DMV?"

"Our contact's gone for the day and I can't get into their files on my own. Well, maybe I could but it'd take a while, and my daddy'd kick my ass if I got arrested for illegal hacking."

"Try checking with the INS, see if Manganaris is a resident alien. They'll have family history if he is."

"Already thought of that. Next up."

She called the local Immigration and Naturalization Service office, went through a glib piece of rigmarole in which she claimed to be personnel director of the agency and needed to know if Harold Manganaris, who had applied for a job with us, had a valid green card and to verify certain information he'd given on his application. Wasted effort. No green card. So he was either a citizen by birth or adoption, or an unregistered alien.

Tamara contacted the Australian embassy, to determine if he had or had ever had a valid Australian passport. They said they'd get back to her, but when five o'clock rolled around they hadn't called. Tamara hadn't found out anything from any other source by then, either.

Which left me with a decision to make. Hanging around, waiting for something to turn up, was playing hell with my nerves, and it would be worse tomorrow. I craved movement, activity. One thing I could do was to drive up to Woodland and have a talk with Grant Johnson, find out if he was in fact hiding useful information about Annette Byers. Fine, but should I make the drive tonight or wait until first thing in the morning? If I left now I'd have to fight commute traffic through the city, across the Bay Bridge, and most of the way on Highway 80 as far as Vacaville—a two-hour trip stretched out into a three-hour-plus one. I just wasn't up to it. Tired from all the running around today, not much sleep the past three nights, still stiff and sore . . . I needed rest more than anything else. The drive would be much easier in the morning, going against the commute. And if Tamara turned up a lead that demanded immediate attention, I could always reverse direction without losing too much time.

Tomorrow, then. Push myself too hard, and I wouldn't be in shape to deal with Manganaris when I finally found him.

Kerry had to work late—I phoned her before I left the office—so I picked up Emily at the Simpsons. They were Diamond Heights neighbors, the Simpsons, whose daughter went to the same school and was the same age. Emily had never had many friends, but she seemed to be slowly forming a bond with Carla Simpson. Encouraging. So was the fact that she seemed to be coping better since our talk Saturday night, no longer quite so frightened or withdrawn.

I made an effort to spend quality time with her this night. She was good with computers, as most kids are these days, and I let her show me some things on her PC. Simple, basic stuff, but I had to admit that I found it of mild interest. Resistance waning a bit? Maybe. I was never going to be a full-fledged convert to modern technology, but even technophobes can get to know the enemy without compromising their principles. I said as much to Emily, and she laughed. That in itself made the computer lesson worthwhile.

I suggested we make dinner and surprise Kerry. She liked the idea, so we put together a meat lasagna and a green salad, messing up the kitchen and then giving it a good cleaning afterward. She was animated the whole time; I heard her laugh again, several times. The way she looked at me tonight, with more love than fear and uncertainty, led me to remember that she'd called me Daddy in that house in Daly City. She hadn't done it again since, but I found myself hoping she would. I wanted to hear her use that word more than I would have thought possible a year or so ago.

Kerry was surprised and pleased when she came home. The good domestic mood lasted through dinner and afterward—all surface cheer, the kind that can be shattered by the wrong word or action, but that didn't happen. On our way back to normal.

Later, when Kerry and I were in bed, I drew her close and said, "I've shut you out the past few days and I feel bad about it. I'm sorry, babe."

"I understand what you're going through."

"I know you do, but you're hurting, too. Selfish and stupid of me not to confide in you. My God, I talked to Emily about what happened. And Tamara knows more than you about what I've been doing since."

"Do you want to talk about it now?"

"Yes," I said, and I told her about Harold Manganaris, how I'd found out about him and what I believed he and Annette Byers had done. Two things I didn't tell her, because I still did not have the right words to express them: the sense of internal bleeding and the constant reminder of the clicks.

She said, "Have you told all of that to the police?"

"Not yet. Not until I get closer to Manganaris."

"How close? You feel you have to confront him?"

"At some point, yes. But not in any physical way—none of that revenge crap. Just to let him know to his face that I helped nail him. And it doesn't have to be before he's arrested. In jail afterward is good enough."

"Then why—?"

Bill Pronzini

"I need to feel I've done everything I possibly can before I step aside. Manganaris and Byers heaped chaos on me, my client, you and Emily by association. The job of bringing them down is as much mine as the system's. It's the only way I'll ever have any peace of mind."

"Closure," Kerry said.

"That's as good a word for it as any."

"And the sooner the better."

"Exactly."

We lay in silence then, holding each other, warmed by each other. I felt that I could sleep tonight, without evil dreams or night sweats. The clicks were there, but they did not seem to be quite as loud. No, not quite as loud.

18

WOODLAND. OLD GOLD RUSH TOWN ON Highway 5 a dozen miles northeast of Davis and twenty miles or so from Sacramento, population around forty thousand, supported these days by light industry and agriculture. Quiet, tree-shaded streets; a premium on Victorian and two-story frame houses on large lots. Sweltering hot in the summer months, but the Sacramento River ran its twisting course a few miles away and offered recreational ways to beat the heat.

It was warm there even for this time of year when I rolled in at ten o'clock. I stopped at a Shell station off the freeway to fuel up and ask directions to Benson Avenue. Fifteen minutes after that I was parked in front of RiteClean Plumbing and Heating and on my way into a sprawling showroom packed with kitchen and bathroom displays and appliances.

I had a story ready to explain my request for an audience with Grant Johnson, but I didn't need to use it. The elderly woman on office duty told me he was taking the day off work.

"What reason did he give?" I asked, making it sound casual.

"Well, a personal matter."

"Nothing serious, I hope."

"I'm sure I don't know."

"Did he call in today or arrange for the time off last night?"

"He called this morning."

I asked the woman how to get to Rio Oso, saying that I would try to reach Johnson at home. She wasn't the suspicious type; she not only obliged, she smiled and wished me a nice day.

Outside in the car, I checked in with Tamara. She said, "Mostly spam this morning."

"Spam?"

"Junk, useless stuff. Computer term."

"Nothing useful?"

"Well, I got his DMV records. California driver's license, renewed three years ago. Duboce address, so that's a dead end. Height: six feet. Weight: two-twenty. Hair and eyes, both brown. Date of birth: June 16, 1959. Place still unknown."

"What kind of car's registered to him?"

"Olds Cutlass, five years old." She read me the license plate number.

"Might still be driving it, might not. One thing's sure—he's not using Byers' MG."

"Uh-uh. Still hasn't been found, by the way. I checked with Felicia. Also no word on Byers, and the cops haven't turned up her connection to Manganaris yet."

"They will eventually," I said. "How about other people with that name? Any in the state?"

"Surprise there. Three—one in L.A., one in Hollister, one in Yreka."

"Could be they're all related in some way."

"That's what I'm digging on now."

"All right, but don't phone any of them. We don't want to alert a relative Manganaris might be in touch with. As far as he knows, no one's ID'ed him as the shooter."

I had a little more difficulty finding Rio Oso than I had Benson

Avenue. It was a one-block cul-de-sac that looped in behind another street in a solidly middle-class neighborhood of older homes. The Johnsons' address was a two-story brown-shingled house with a porch that wrapped half around on one side. A gnarled old black walnut provided shade in front and on the porch side. The driveway and the curb in front were empty, but I could see a garage in back and the doors were shut.

Nobody answered the doorbell. I thought about walking up the drive to check the garage, decided that wasn't such a good idea in a neighborhood like this, and went back to the car. Wait awhile, see if anybody showed up? It was either that or talk to the neighbors, and I was not ready to try that yet. But waiting here, one man alone in a parked car, was a bad idea for the same reason as trespassing. Better to go away somewhere for a time and then come back.

I drove around until I spotted a strip mall that had a cafe in it. Breakfast had been a cup of coffee and a glass of orange juice, so I sat in there and drank more coffee and ate eggs and toast that I didn't particularly want. That used up half an hour. I made myself linger another ten minutes before I climbed back into the car and returned to Rio Oso.

The Johnson driveway was occupied now, by a dark blue SUV that must have just pulled in. The driver's door was open, and a blonde woman in Levi's and a white shirt was balancing a baby in one arm and using the other to open one of those fold-up strollers they have nowadays. A little boy of about four skipped around beside her; from a distance it looked as though he was performing some sort of ritual dance.

I parked, walked over there and up the drive. The woman looked startled when she saw me; the boy stopped his dance and stared with big round eyes like a kid in a Keane painting. I said through what I hoped was a disarming smile, "Mrs. Johnson?"

"Yes? What is it?" She was about twenty-five, big-boned, and attractive. But the Levi's were a mistake, pointing up the fact that she had heavy thighs and broad hips.

"I need to talk to your husband. Can you tell me—"

"What do you want with Grant?" Wary and nervous, both.

In the detective business you learn to read people quickly and to make snap decisions in how to handle them. Game-playing would not get me anywhere with Melanie Johnson. A direct, straightforward approach was the one chance I had at cooperation from her. I unpocketed my wallet, doing it slowly so as not to alarm her, and flipped open to the photostat of my investigator's license. I said my name at the same time I showed her the license.

She went pale. Her mouth opened, closed, opened again, fishlike, before she said, "You . . . you're the detective who was almost. . . ."

"Almost murdered in Daly City. That's right."

"Oh, God. What do you . . . why are you *here?*"

"To see your husband, as I said."

"Why? Grant doesn't know anything about that. He's a good man; he never hurt anyone in his life."

"I don't doubt that."

"Then what do you want with him? For Lord's sake, we have a family, little children. . . ."

"I mean no harm to you or your husband or your family, Mrs. Johnson. Information is all I'm after."

"I told you, he doesn't know—"

"Annette Byers," I said.

She caught her breath. Made a little sound in her throat and said, "Oh, God," again.

"How long has it been since you've seen her?"

"I've never seen her. That was all over before Grant and I met. I don't know that bitch, I don't want anything to do with her."

"How long since your husband saw her last?"

The baby in the stroller set up a sudden wailing. The little boy moved over and hugged his mother's leg. Melanie Johnson looked at the infant, at the boy, at the SUV, at the house, at the street— everywhere but at me. The beginnings of panic glistened in her eyes, created a twitch at one corner of her mouth.

"I meant what I said about no harm to you. Finding Annette Byers and the man she's with is the only reason I'm here. If you have any idea where they are, I'd advise you to tell me now. It might save you a visit from the police later on."

The baby yowled louder. Mrs. Johnson said almost desperately, "She needs changing. We can't talk out here . . . the neighbors . . . I can't think with her screaming like that."

"Inside would be better," I agreed. "Were you just out shopping?"

"What? Oh, shopping, yes. . . ."

I gestured at the SUV. "Groceries inside?"

"Yes, but. . . ."

"You go ahead with your kids. I'll bring the groceries."

My offer eased the panic in her; the look she flashed me was more stunned than frightened. She nodded, turned to push the stroller toward the front walk, the four-year-old clinging to her leg. I opened the SUV's rear door, hauled out four large bags of food and paper products, and lugged them onto the porch. She had the front door open by then; I followed her inside.

The house was cluttered with toys but otherwise reasonably well kept. She said, "The kitchen's this way," and led me out there. I put the groceries on the sink counter while she lifted the squalling infant from the stroller. "I have to change her right away. She gets a rash if she's wet too long."

"All right."

We went back into the toy-strewn living room. She said distract-edly, "Will you watch Michael while I change the baby?"

"Sure."

She told the boy to sit down, took the infant into another room. I leaned a hip on the arm of a recliner and watched Michael watch me with his big round eyes. After a time, when the baby's yowls sub-sided, I winked at him and made a rocking gesture with folded arms. All that got me was a pooch face. I treated him to one of my own in return. He stuck out his tongue; I did the same. He was giggling and mugging at me like Red Skelton when his mother returned.

She said, "You're good with him. Do you have children?"

"One adopted daughter. She's ten."

"My other son is adopted. He's in kindergarten now." Her mouth quirked. "Grant's son by that bitch. But I guess you know that."

"Yes."

"I love Kevin like he's my own, I really do. I'm the only mother he's ever had. She never wanted anything to do with him. Or with Grant anymore until. . . ."

"Until when, Mrs. Johnson?"

She sat heavily on a corduroy sofa. Michael ran over and hopped up beside her and laid his head in her lap. She stroked his dark-blond hair absently as she said, "I want to tell you, but I don't know . . . I shouldn't say anything without Grant being here."

"Do you know where he is now?"

"At work. I'd better call him. . . ."

"He's not at work," I said.

"He . . . what? He's not?"

"I stopped by RiteClean Plumbing before I came here. The woman in the office said he was taking the day off to attend to personal business. Called in about it this morning."

"Oh, God," she said.

"He didn't say anything to you?"

"No. He . . . no, not a word."

"Where do you suppose he went?"

She shook her head.

"To see Annette Byers?"

"He saw her yesterday. He said we didn't have to worry, she was leaving right away."

"Start at the beginning, Mrs. Johnson. Make it easier on both of us."

She drew a breath before she said, "That woman called here last week. Out of the blue . . . Grant swore it was the first time he'd heard from her since she gave up custody of Kevin. He wasn't lying. He was as surprised as I was—I could see it in his eyes."

"What day was that?"

"Saturday. Early Saturday morning."

"Where was she calling from?"

"She wouldn't say."

"Purpose of the call?"

"She wanted a place to stay for a week or two. She said she was having problems with an abusive boyfriend, had no one else to turn to."

"She wanted to stay here, in your house?"

"Lord, no. She wouldn't dare have asked that. Grant has a fishing shack on the river that belonged to his father."

"Sacramento River?"

"Yes. Up beyond Knight's Landing. She knew about it from when they were . . . seeing each other, hoped he'd still have it." Melanie Johnson's mouth flexed and tightened, as if she were tasting bile. "He used to take her there. I wouldn't be surprised if it was where Kevin was conceived."

"What was your husband's reaction to her request?"

"He didn't want anything to do with her, after all this time. But she begged him . . . she was crying; he said she really sounded terrified. Grant has a soft heart . . . too soft sometimes. He gave in. I guess I can't blame him. He said she could stay at the shack as long as she kept away from us, from Kevin. He told her where he hides the key so he wouldn't have to see her."

"Just her staying at the shack, no one else?"

"That's what she said."

"Did either of you hear from her again?"

"No. But then we read in the papers that the police were looking for her, that she was mixed up in that murder case. And yesterday a San Francisco newspaper reporter called Grant and asked about her. It scared us. If the police found her at the shack, we were afraid Grant would be arrested, too . . . aiding a fugitive or something."

"So what did you decide to do?"

"Grant said the best thing was to tell her she couldn't stay any longer, make her leave if he had to. There's no phone at the shack, so he drove up yesterday afternoon after work."

"And?"

"She didn't give him any trouble, he said. Agreed to leave right away. But he was gone a long time, and he seemed upset when he came home."

"Did you ask him about that?"

"Yes. He said it was painful seeing her again, and he stopped for a couple of beers afterward." She paused and then said, "Only now you tell me he's not at work today. If he went back up there . . . why would he do that?"

The question was for herself, not me. I said nothing.

"I don't understand it. He's not a liar, really he's not. We've never had any secrets from each other. He'd never start up with that bitch again, I know he wouldn't . . . But now that I think about it, his breath didn't smell of beer last night. . . ."

I was not going there with her. I said, "There's probably a simple explanation, Mrs. Johnson," and then I asked, "Where exactly is the fishing shack?"

She told me; it sounded easy enough to find. Then she said, "You have to tell me something now. How much trouble is my husband in? *Can* he be arrested for aiding a fugitive?"

"Not if everything you've told me is the truth." And if he hadn't been helping her in some other way, last night and/or today.

"It's the truth, believe me." She sighed heavily. "He'll be mad at me for talking to you like this."

"You did the right thing, Mrs. Johnson."

She lifted Michael's thin body, hugged him so tight against her breast he began to squirm. "Yes," she said a little grimly, "I know I did."

I crossed the Sacramento River on Highway 113 out of Woodland. The Sacramento is a big river, 375 miles of loops and bends and white-water rapids from its headwaters near Mount Shasta to San Francisco Bay; an important river in terms of agribusiness, transportation, the endangered Chinook salmon; a controversial river for the ongoing, often bitter struggles over water use, pollution control, and its fragile ecosystem; a badly used river by logging, mining, manufacturing, developmental, and political interests. But you might not guess any of that if you saw it for the first time from the bridge at Knight's Landing. From there the Sacramento looks small, tame, insignificant—a none too appetizing muddy brown, glinting under the rays of the midday sun.

Along the rivercourse south of Knight's Landing is where Sacramento's gentry live in expensive ranch-style homes and pink-and-white estate villas, their pleasure boats kept in ritzy marinas; north of the village is not much of anything except open grassland and wetland, a fifty-mile stretch up to Colusa that unrestricted logging has all but denuded of the riparian forests that once grew along there. Grant Johnson's fishing shack was in that stretch, a few miles upriver.

Highway 113 continues northeast to Yuba City, but at a wide spot called Robbins, Melanie Johnson had told me, a back road branches off to parallel the river. I found it and followed it a couple of miles to where a rutted track angled over to the river hamlet of Kirkville. Look for a dirt lane just outside Kirkville, she'd told me. I looked, spotted it, turned, and jounced along its narrow, snaky length for a tenth of a mile until I could see the river again.

That was far enough in the car. I left it sitting in the middle of the lane, not because the track was little used, but to block any potential escape. Before I got out, I checked the loads in the .38 and put the weapon in my pocket.

I walked ahead slowly, keening the way an animal does. Blackbirds chattered in a line of bushes that partially blocked my view of the river; there was no other sound that I could hear. A gusty little wind brought the water smell to me, a good, fresh smell in spite of its muddiness.

The bushes helped screen my approach. When I reached them, I had a clear look at the river, a few hundred yards wide at this point, and part of the near shoreline. Stunted willows, wild grape, and three tumbledown, board-and-batten shacks squatting at the water's edge at fifty-yard intervals. Two of the shacks had stubby, rotting piers jutting from their backsides; the one I wanted was the second of the the two, the farthest upriver. From where I stood, I could see only its outer half. I eased ahead a pace at a time until the bushes thinned and the rest of it came into sight.

The front of the shack had two steps leading up to the door. A man was sitting on the top one, hunched forward, elbows on knees and chin on the backs of his hands. Brown-haired, brown-bearded, and unfamiliar—Grant Johnson, no doubt, because the pickup truck parked nearby had the words RiteClean Plumbing and Heating on the driver's door.

But what tightened the muscles in my neck and shoulders, my fingers around the .38's grip, was neither Johnson nor his truck. It was the other car parked there, drawn up close on the shack's far side.

Annette Byers' MG.

19

I GOT TO WITHIN THIRTY YARDS OF THE SHACK before the wind lulled and Johnson heard or sensed my presence. His head jerked up; then he was on his feet in one awkward lunge. He was linebacker big, going soft around the middle but with the kind of size and muscle that would make him rough goods in a fight. If he'd made any sort of move in my direction, I would have had to show him the gun. But he was not the aggressive type. He stood swaying slightly, slump-shouldered, gawping at me out of widened eyes, his face twisted with anguish and confusion.

"Who the hell're you?" he said in rumbly tones.

I told him who I was, name and profession both. Recognition brought a grimace and the words, "Oh, God." Favorite Johnson family phrase in times of stress, as if it were an invocation for first aid.

"Where's Annette Byers?"

I was prepared for lies or evasions; I got neither. He said, "Inside. Asleep, unconscious . . . I don't know."

"Alone?"

"Yeah. She's hurt, sick. . . ."

"Hurt how?"

"Somebody beat her up. She wouldn't say who . . . the guy she was mixed up with, I guess, the bald guy they wrote about in the papers. I think she's got internal injuries . . . she's been puking up blood."

"How long has she been like that?"

"Awhile. Before she came here on Saturday."

"You were here last night. For Christ's sake, why didn't you take her to a hospital?"

His eyelids slatted. "How'd you know I was here last night? How'd you find out about me, this place?"

"Never mind that. Answer the question. Why didn't you take her to a hospital?"

"I wanted to, but she wouldn't let me. She said the cops would arrest her for murder, arrest me for harboring a fugitive. She's so damn scared . . . I couldn't force her to go. I've got my family to think of. And Annette, she's the mother of my oldest son. You understand?"

I understood, all right. I'd heard it all before, in one form or another, and I didn't like it any better this time than I had the others.

"She gave me some money," Johnson said, " a lot of money . . . she wanted me to buy her drugs. Methamphetamines, cocaine, morphine, whatever I could get. She's strung out, real bad."

"Did you make a buy for her? That why you came back up here today?"

"No. I couldn't do it. I know a guy, but . . . I hate drugs, I hate what they do to people. I came back to tell her I couldn't, that the only thing I could do for her was take her to a doctor." He raked hooked fingers through his beard, making a raspy sound that was audible above the thrum of the wind. "She . . . went crazy. Called me all kinds of names, tried to claw my face. Then all of a sudden she passed out."

"How long ago was that?"

"Twenty minutes, half an hour. I couldn't wake her up, so I came out here to think. Decide what to do."

"Well now you won't have to do any more thinking. I'll make the decision for you."

"What decision? What're you gonna do?"

"Go inside and have a look at her, first. You wait here."

He started to argue, changed his mind, and stepped aside to let me pass. Soft-hearted, his wife had called him. Soft-headed, too, for all his bulk: weak, indecisive, ineffectual in a crisis. I pitied his family in any other emergency that might come up in their lives.

The shack was one room, maybe fifteen feet square, dim because the single window overlooking the river was tightly shuttered. There were shelves and an ancient icebox on one wall, a table and two chairs in the middle of the bare floor, and a double tier of bunk beds against another wall. No cooking facilities, a chemical toilet in a doorless alcove, a space heater near the bunks that was turned on but didn't throw out much heat. The air in there held a chill, smelled rawly of sickness and human waste.

Annette Byers was on the lower bunk, a curled mound hidden under a skimpy blanket. I went over and eased the blanket down so I could see her face. An unhealthy white stained with fever blotches and a purple-yellow bruise on the exposed temple; pain lines deeply etched around her mouth, the lips so cracked there were spots of blood where the fissures had opened. She moaned, flopped over on her back, but her eyes stayed shut. I laid the back of my hand on her forehead. Hot. One of her hands was clear of the blanket; I lifted it, held it for a few seconds. Her pulse was weak, fluttery.

Johnson had said she might have internal injuries, so I drew the blanket down far enough to have a look at her torso. Jesus. She wore a T-shirt and panties, and the shirt had hiked up under her breasts; a solid pattern of bruises covered most of the exposed skin across her belly and abdomen. Heavy blows to that part of a woman's body could easily rupture the spleen, damage other organs, and cause internal bleeding.

She moaned again, shivering. I recovered her, and as I did, the lower edge of the blanket came loose from around her feet and I noticed the bulge of something down there, wedged partway between the bunk and the wall. I knew what it was even before I got a grip on it and dragged it out.

Jay Cohalan's cowhide briefcase.

The weight of it said it was full; I unfastened the catches and looked inside just long enough to verify the contents. The money, all right. A few of the packets torn open, the rest intact. Most if not all of the seventy-five thousand. Even as hurt and sick as she was, she'd kept it close the whole time she was here—slept with it, maybe fondled it to help ease her suffering. The damn money to these people was the world, the universe, God and the devil both.

I looked around for something else to cover her with, keep her warm. Nothing. The space heater was turned up as high as it would go; I moved it a little closer to the bunk. Then I snugged up the case and took it outside with me.

Johnson was pacing around on the grass in front. He stopped when he saw me. The briefcase didn't seem to register on him; his gaze held on mine.

"She awake now?"

"No."

"You think she'll be all right?"

"If you'd gotten her medical attention last night, she'd have a hell of a lot better chance than she does now. That truck of yours equipped with a mobile phone?"

"Yeah."

"Go put in an emergency medical call. Tell them where we are and to get an ambulance or a medivac helicopter out here as fast as they can."

"Can't we just take her to a hospital?"

"It's too late to risk moving her. Do what I told you, no arguments."

He bobbed his head. "Should I tell them her name?"

"Might as well. They'd find it out pretty soon anyway. But you don't need to say anything about me, now or later. I won't be here when the medics and the law arrive. Take all the credit for yourself."

"Credit," he said. "Oh, God, I hope she doesn't die. I loved her once, she's Kevin mother. I couldn't stand that on my conscience. . . ."

"Goddamn it, make that call."

He hurried away to the pickup. I went in the opposite direction at a trot, opened the car's trunk, traded the briefcase for the blanket I keep in there. I could have left the money in the shack for the authorities to find, maybe should have; but it had been my responsibility, and at least some of this mess would not have happened if I'd been more careful. I was not about to walk away from it now that I had control of it again.

I drove to the shack, turned the car around there. Johnson was still in his truck. I took the blanket inside, tucked it around Byers' trembling body. She'd become restless, moving her head from side to side, making noises in her throat. Some of them were words, but I couldn't make sense of them. Delirious. I'd had the idea of trying to wake her up, see if I could get her to answer some questions, but here with her again it seemed futile and risky.

Her suede shoulder bag was on the top bunk. I dumped out the contents, pawed through them. The usual stuff, and the only item of interest a dog-eared address book. Dingo was listed in there, under that name alone, with the Duboce Street address and an old phone number scratched out and new ones inked in—Pueblo Street in the city. That must be where he'd been living recently. Would he be holed up there? Possible, but not likely. The other names and addresses told me nothing, but there were a few I didn't recognize. I pocketed the book, scooped the rest of the stuff back into the bag.

"No!"

The sudden cry made me jump a little. When I looked at her, her eyes were wide open and red-flecked drool crawled from the corner of her mouth. But she was not seeing me or anything else in the room. She muttered something that I couldn't make out, then began babbling in fits and starts. I sank to one knee, leaned my head close enough to her mouth to feel and smell the sour warmth of her breath.

"Stop it stop it stop it . . . crazy bastard what's the matter with you, leave me alone! Dirty son of a bitch!" Incoherent. "How d'you like it huh? How d'you like getting hit you sick creep . . . break your fuckin' head open. . . ." Incoherent. "Oh shit what am I gonna do now . . . kill me if he finds me . . ." Incoherent. "Please . . . hurts so much . . . puking up blood he must've broke something inside. . . ." Incoherent. "I've got to have it for the pain . . . something anything please Grant please. . . ." A series of whimpers, more sentence fragments, as if a nightmare scene kept replaying on a loop in her head.

I'd heard enough. Had enough in here. I straightened, made sure the blankets covered her completely, and then went back outside and shut the door behind me.

Johnson was standing there, running his hands up and down his sides as if trying to cleanse them. He said, "They're on the way."

"Make sure you wait for them. And make sure you forget I was here."

"I will. What're you gonna do?"

"Find the man who hurt her like that."

"Then what?"

"That depends on him. Did she say anything about him? Where he might be?"

"No."

"Mention the name Dingo at any time?"

"Once. She said if Dingo found her he'd kill her."

"She tell you where she was before she came here? Where he beat her up?"

"No. She wouldn't talk about any of that."

I brushed past him, went to the MG. The driver's door wasn't locked. Spots of dried blood on the driver's bucket; nothing else on any of the seats. And nothing on the floorboards or among the clutter in the glove box. I pulled the trunk release and looked in there. Nothing.

Johnson was still rooted in the same spot. "All right," I said to him, "I'm going now. Stay inside with her until somebody comes. Keep her warm, don't let her kick the blankets off."

"I'll take care of her," he said.

Sure you will, I thought. Just like you've been taking care of her since last night. You soft-hearted, compassionate tower of strength you.

20

I WAS IN A FOUL HUMOR BY THE TIME I GOT back to the city. I could not shake the feeling that I'd abandoned Annette Byers, left Grant Johnson holding an empty bag. Irrational on both counts. Byers, for Christ's sake, was an extortionist, a thief, an accessory to the murders of Carolyn Dain and Jay Cohalan and the near-murder of me. Cold, ruthless, mercenary, badly screwed up on drugs—nobody to feel sorry for. Unless you'd seen her lying there with the red drool coming out of her mouth, the savage bruises on her belly and abdomen, the evident internal damage. A scared, battered, pain-wracked kid—that was the image I'd carried away with me. And Johnson, for all his shortcomings, was another scared kid with a dependent wife and three little kids of his own. Yeah, I felt bad. But not bad enough to turn around and go back at any point, or to relinquish custodianship of the money.

If I was reading correctly what Byers had said in her delirium, she and Manganaris had had some sort of falling out—over the seventy-five thousand, likely—and he'd gone to work on her with his fists. Might have ended up killing her just as he'd killed the others, except that she'd managed to turn the tables somehow, put him out of commission long enough to escape with the briefcase. It was possible she'd made *him* dead, but I didn't want to believe it. If she had, she wouldn't have gone begging to a former lover she hadn't seen in years, all scared and desperate; she could have holed up anywhere and felt safe enough. Fear of the police alone wasn't enough to have sent her into hiding in that isolated fishing shack. Fear of Manganaris was.

And where was Manganaris? Out somewhere hunting for her? Hiding at the Pueblo Street address? Wherever he was, he had to be in a frenzy of hate, rage, frustration. And if he was using meth or some other drug, he was worse than a madman on the loose—he was a walking time bomb.

Oh, they were some pair, Byers and Dingo. Set up a bleeder scam, doublecross Cohalan, murder two people in cold blood, doublecross each other, do physical harm to each other—all for seventy-five thousand dollars that neither of them had held onto for very long and would never touch again. Senseless from start to finish. Crazy. And I was feeling a thin worm of pity for her? Hell, that made me crazy, too, didn't it?

I drove straight to O'Farrell, took the briefcase upstairs to the office. Tamara's mood was little better than mine; her computer had crashed, been down for nearly three hours, and she'd only just gotten it up and working again. So she had nothing more for me on Manganaris, nothing yet on the other three who shared the name.

While I locked the stacks of cash in the safe for the second time, I told her about Byers and Johnson. She had only two questions.

"What'll you do if Johnson tells the law about you being at the shack?"

"I don't think he will. But if he does I'll stand up to the heat when the time comes. I can't worry about it now."

"And the money, what about that?"

"I don't know yet. I doubt Johnson noticed my taking the briefcase, and Byers wouldn't have let him see it or any more of the money than what she gave him for drugs. Maybe I'll turn it over to Fuentes or Craddock. Maybe I'll contact Mel Bishop and ask him if Carolyn Dain had a favorite charity and donate the money anonymously in her name. She had no living relatives."

"Better some charity than the damn state," Tamara said.

"Probably. But I just don't know yet."

The Pueblo Street address was an antiquated chipped-stucco apartment building in a low-income Visitacion Valley neighborhood across from the Cow Palace. Manganaris seemed to have downscaled rather than upscaled his standard of living when he moved. Or maybe he just hadn't liked living in one place too long, cared little about his surroundings, and took whatever rental came along cheap.

Once I'd pinpointed the building, I drove around several blocks on the lookout for an Olds Cutlass. I spotted one, but it was the wrong year and had the wrong license plate. For all I knew, he was driving something else now, but it pays to cover all the bases.

I parked around the corner on Geneva and went to the building on foot, the .38 in my coat pocket and my hand wrapped around it. There was an iron-barred security gate, but it wasn't locked; all I had to do was push it open and walk in. Some building. Byers' address book had Dingo's apartment number as 302. The elevator looked creaky and unreliable, and I did not want to be closed up in anything that small here. I climbed two flights of stairs that stank of Lysol and urine. Some half-wit had fastened a condom around the knob atop one of the railings; the walls were decorated with similarly unfunny sexual references and the inexplicable marks of taggers.

The third-floor hallway had a different odor: the olfactory remnants of somebody's Mexican dinner cooked in lard. Mouth-breathing, walking on the balls of my feet, I eased my way along to 302. Laid an ear close to the thin door panel, heard nothing, and then flattened back against the wall next to the door and reached out to rap on the wood with my left hand. I had the gun halfway clear of my pocket as I waited.

No answer. No sound.

I tried again, got more of the same, and dropped my free hand to the doorknob. It turned freely. The only way to tell if that meant something or nothing was to go in there, fast and low, with the gun extended. I held a breath, started to open the door.

"Hey, you over there."

Woman's voice, behind me. I snapped my head around, letting go of the knob, shoving the .38 down out of sight. She hadn't seen the weapon; she was in the doorway of an apartment across and down the hall, 305, and she stayed there when I turned to face her.

I put on a smile that felt tight and strained. "Yes, ma'am?"

"He ain't there," she said. "That crazy cueball better not show his face around here again, he knows what's good for him. You wouldn't be a cop?"

"Not exactly."

"What's that mean, not exactly?"

"I'm not a cop."

"Relative of the cueball's or what?"

"No. Business matter."

"Business." She snorted through her nose, a sound like a goose honking. "Monkey business, hah?"

I relaxed a little and moved over to where she stood. She was close to seventy, her round red face a mass of folds and seams like an apple that had been desiccated by the elements. Stringy gray-black hair lay in flat, sparse curls on a dandruff-flecked scalp. She wore a chenille bathrobe that looked as old as she was, and even at a distance of three feet I could tell that she had a fondness for sweet wine.

"He owes me something," I said.

"Money?"

"Not anymore. When did you see him last?"

"Night I called the cops on him, that's when."

"What night was that?"

"Last Friday night. Hell, Saturday morning—three A.M."

"Why? What happened?"

"What didn't happen, you mean. Cussing, yelling, screaming, shooting, you name it. Woke up the whole damn building."

"Shooting?"

"Fired a gun over there. Boom! I know a gunshot when I hear one."

"Manganaris and a woman, is that right?"

"That's what I told the cops. Him and his dolly, fighting, busting up the furniture, her screaming like a banshee. Then the gun went off, boom! and pretty quick she come running out like the devil himself was after her. I had my door cracked by then, and I saw her."

"Was she carrying anything? A briefcase?"

"Had something in one hand, might've been a briefcase. All doubled over, clutching her middle. I didn't see no blood, though. I don't think she was shot."

"What about him?"

"He come staggering out four minutes and eleven seconds after she did. I timed it on my clock."

"Staggering, you said. Was he shot?"

"Didn't see no blood on him, neither. But he was spitting cusswords and holding his head. I hope she did shoot him. Serve that crazy cueball right for beating up women, wrecking a decent person's sleep."

"He been back here since?"

"Better not come back. I'll call the cops again if he does, file another complaint against him."

"You're sure he hasn't been here, even once?"

"Sure I'm sure." Then she frowned, snorted, and breathed more cream sherry fumes at me. "What kind of question is that? You think I got nothing better to do than spy on my neighbors?"

"I didn't mean it that way. . . ."

"I'll have you know I'm a respectable woman who minds her own business," she said with haughty indignation and retreated into her apartment and slammed the door.

I walked soft to 302, eased the door open and myself inside, the .38 drawn in spite of what the woman had said. The apartment was two rooms of tasteless bargain-basement furniture, empty beer and wine bottles, the rotting remains of a couple of take-out meals. There'd been a fight in here, all right. Tables and chairs were askew, the shards of a ceramic lamp and cigarette butts from an upended ashtray littered the threadbare carpet, a cheap picture had been knocked off one wall and its glass splintered in the drop. There was a scorched hole in one of the sofa cushions that was large enough to have been made by a bullet; I dug around in the foam-rubber padding and found the slug, examined it briefly for traces of blood. Didn't seem to be any. If Annette Byers had fired the gun, she'd evidently missed. Or possibly they'd struggled over it, and it had discharged that way. She must have smacked Manganaris with something—the gun, that busted lamp, one of the empty wine bottles—to put him down for those four minutes and eleven seconds.

There was nothing else for me in the living room, or in the pocket-size kitchenette, or in the equally tiny bathroom. In the bedroom, the sheets on the double bed were soiled and wadded together. The top of the single nightstand held an overflowing ashtray and a glass stained with red wine residue; the drawer under it was empty except for an opened package of condoms and a well-used crack pipe. The crack pipe said the police hadn't bothered to search carefully; the fact that the door had been left unlocked confirmed their sloppy handling of the complaint.

The drawers in the bureau contained nothing that held my attention. Closet next. A few shirts and pants and a denim jacket on hangers, a pile of soiled clothing on the floor. Manganaris hadn't spent much of his income, legal or illegal, on clothes or luxury items; most had probably gone for drugs, alcohol, tobacco, and food. The only other item in the closet was a battered old sailor's duffel bag. It didn't make him ex-navy or ex-merchant marine; you could buy duffels like that one in any army-navy store. At first I thought it was empty, but when I brushed my hand over an inside zipper compartment, something made a crinkly sound. I fished it out.

An old nine-by-twelve color photograph, wrinkled and torn along a couple of its edges. Posed group shot of a high school football team decked out in green-and-gold uniforms. A two-line boldface caption read:

EAST CENTRAL VALLEY TIGERCATS
1976 CONFERENCE CHAMPIONS

Below that was a list of names, but the type was tiny and the light too poor in there for me to make them out. I took the photo into the bathroom, which had a stronger bulb, and used the little gadget magnifying glass on my keychain to scan the names. Second row, third from the left: Harold "Mean Joe" Manganaris. I squinted at the face that went with it. Yeah. He'd had all his hair then, but the bushy eyebrows and the snarling mouth were the same.

There was nothing on the front or back of the photo to tell me where East Central Valley High School was located. Tamara's meat. I went back to the living room, to the phone I'd seen in there. It was still operational; I used it to call the agency. No problem, Tamara said, as long as East Central Valley was a California school. The State Board of Education would have a complete list. She'd know one way or another in a few minutes.

I folded the photograph, tucked it into my coat pocket, and let myself out. The mummified minder of her own business was peering out through her front door again. She said, "Hey, what you been doing in there? You ain't got no right to be in there."

"The door was unlocked."

"Yeah? I thought those cops locked it when they were done poking around in there Friday night."

"Evidently not."

"You still ain't got no right to be in there. That crazy cueball finds out, he won't like it."

"I don't care what he likes or doesn't like," I said. "I told you, he owes me."

"You didn't steal nothing, did you?"

"No. There's nothing worth stealing."

"You sure about that? Nothing at all?"

"Why don't you go over and have a look for yourself?"

She didn't like that; she made a catlike spitting noise as I went past her and yelled at my back, "I ain't that kind! I don't trespass on other people's property! Who you think you are anyway? I ought to call the cops on you!" She was still ranting as I went through the door to the stairwell.

I had just unlocked my car when the mobile phone went off. Tamara. Fast service—and the news was good. Very good.

"East Central Valley High's a small school on the outskirts of Hollister," she said.

"Hollister. Didn't you tell me one of the other Manganarises lived there?"

"Near there, right. Mr. Adam Manganaris."

"Address for him yet?"

She had one. Not much else on the man, but now that she knew about the school connection, she'd be able to ferret out any relationship between Harold Manganaris and his Hollister namesake.

Son and father.

It took Tamara just half an hour to turn up that information, and I was already on the road by then, heading south down 101. My gut feeling had been son and father; it felt right, and it was right. And where does a man like Dingo go, a man with no friends and no job and little or no cash left to feed his drug habit and no idea where to find Byers or the seventy-five thousand blood money and nowhere else to turn . . . where is he likely to go, at least for a short while, to regroup and refinance?

He goes home.

To his father's place, the Outback Oasis, on Highway 152 east of Hollister.

21

IT WAS ONE OF THOSE LITTLE CROSSROADS spots you still find occasionally in the California backcountry, several miles east of Hollister on the way to the Pinnacles National Monument. Relics of another era; old dying things with precious little time left before they crumble or are bulldozed to make room for something new and not half as appealing. Weathered wooden store building, gas pumps, a detached service garage, some warped little tourist cabins clustered close behind; a couple of junk-car husks and a stand of shade trees. Its name, Outback Oasis, was spelled out on a pocked metal sign on the store roof. There were four cabins, and the shade trees were cottonwoods.

I expected it to be closed by the time I got there at 7:15, but that wasn't the case. Lights showed inside the store, and a big Open sign was displayed in the front window. Sodium vapor lights and the powdery white shine from a nearly full moon sharpened details and created pockets of deep shadow. The cabins were dark except for night lights over the entrances.

No cars were visible back there, and the parking apron was

deserted. I pulled up on the near side of the pumps, outside the pooled glare of the sodium vapor arcs, and sat there for a time, flexing cramped muscles and rubbing away eye grit. I was dead tired and drum tight from all the long-haul driving, the buildup of tension. Close to the end of it now. You get so you can feel it, more a kind of bone-deep ache than conscious intuition. Maybe not here, maybe not tonight or tomorrow, but soon. Soon.

I'd put the Colt back in its dash clip, as I always do when driving; I removed it yet again, held it balanced in the palm of my hand. God, I was sick of that gun, its cold, slick surfaces and its deadly contents. The more I carried it with me into uncertain circumstances, the greater the odds that I'd be forced to use it. I did not want to shoot Harold Manganaris; it would rip me up, keep me bleeding, if he died by my hand and my gun. Yet the driving need to find and confront him was as powerful as ever.

This time I tucked the .38 into my belt at the small of my back. I preferred not to carry a weapon that way, but the front sight had a tendency to hang up in my pocket; and unless I kept my fingers around it, it made conspicuous bulge besides. Hold a gun in your hand long enough, and it can turn you paranoid, increase your inclination to use it.

A warm, dry breeze, heavy with the scents of earth and dry grass, greeted me when I stepped out. In the distance, moonlight made black cutout shapes of the hills of the Diablo Range. It was flat here, and dust-blown, and quiet. The feeling I had was one of isolation, emptiness, displacement in time. Normally I would not have minded that; I like touching the past, the sense of history that seems to elude most people these days. But tonight it served only to whet the edges in me.

It was too warm inside the store. Wood fire crackling inside an ancient pot-bellied stove, despite the fact that the night held no hint of chill. The air had a stale, hanging quality that was heavy in the lungs. The old man behind the counter at the rear had the same leaden aspect. He was slumped on a stool, studying a book of some kind that was open on the countertop. A bell had tinkled to announce my arrival, but at first he didn't look up. As I crossed the room, he turned a page; it made a dry rustling sound. The page was black, with what appeared to be photographs and paper items affixed to it. A scrapbook.

When I reached him, he shut the book. It had a brown, simulated leather cover, the word *Memories* embossed on it in gilt. The gilt had flaked and faded, the ersatz leather was cracked: the scrapbook was almost as old as he was. Over seventy, I judged. Thin, stoop-shouldered, white hair as fine as rabbit fur. Deeply seamed face. Bent left arm that was also knobbed and crooked at the wrist, as if it had been badly broken once and hadn't healed properly. When he finally raised his head, his rheumy gray eyes held weariness and something else that I could not define.

"Evening," he said. Torpid voice, too. "Help you?"

"Are you Adam Manganaris?"

"I am." His accent was discernible but faint, blurred by his years on U.S. soil; if I hadn't known he was Australian, I might not have been able to identify it.

I told him who I was. Nothing changed in his face or eyes, yet I had the sense that he recognized my name. I tried to give him one of my business cards; he wouldn't take it. So I laid it on the counter, face up, and pushed it toward him. He pretended it wasn't there.

"I'm looking for your son, Mr. Manganaris."

No response. His gaze held steady on mine.

"Is he here?"

No response.

"Been here recently?"

No response.

"How long since you've seen or heard from him?"

He said slowly, "I have no son."

"Harold. Also known as Dingo."

No response.

"He's in trouble. The worst kind of trouble."

Face like a chunk of eroded limestone, eyes like cloudy imbedded agates. "I have no son," he said again.

Enough pussyfooting around. I did not want to hurt the old man, but I'd been hurt too much myself to pull any punches. If the brutal approach was the only way to rouse answers out of him, then that was the one I'd use and the hell with it.

"Do you read the San Francisco papers, Mr. Manganaris?"

"No."

"Sure you do. You also watch TV, I'll bet. You know there's an ongoing police investigation involving two murders and the theft of seventy-five thousand dollars in cash entrusted to my care. You also know that I came close to being a third murder victim myself."

Silence.

"The man who pulled the trigger on me and on Carolyn Dain and Jay Cohalan is your son. Like it or not, that's God's honest truth."

Not a flicker of reaction.

"Harold and a woman named Annette Byers planned the whole thing. They had the cash for a while, but neither of them has it any more. She's already in custody. It's only a matter of time until he's caught, but I want to see it happen before anyone else dies or gets hurt."

Silence.

"I think there's a good chance he came here," I said. "You're his father and the only person who can give him what he needs— money, shelter, a place to hide out."

Adam Manganaris pushed off his stool in slow, arthritic movements, picked up the scrapbook and laid it on a shelf behind him. Several regular hardback books lined the rest of the shelf, all of them old and well read.

"Aiding and abetting a fugitive is a felony," I said to his back. "What's the sense in getting yourself in trouble with the law, too? Tell me where he is. It's the best thing for you, the best thing for your son."

Without turning: "How many times do I have to tell you, mate? I have no son."

"In one of the cabins out back, maybe? A fugitive could hole up there for a while if he was careful."

"None of the cabins is occupied."

"How about I go out there and have a look?"

"I can't stop you, can I."

"No, you can't."

I left him and went outside. A big rig pounded past on the highway; otherwise I had the night to myself. I crossed to the closed-up service garage, tried the doors. Secure. There were two windows in the near-side wall, both dusty and speckled with ground-in dirt. I held my pencil flash up to the glass of one, but the light reflected off as much as penetrated the opaque surface. Same thing at the other window. I could make out the shapes of two vehicles inside, but that was all. It was impossible to determine makes or models.

The stand of cottonwoods grew beyond the garage and an unpaved road that led back to the cabins. I moved over into the trees, made my way behind the two cabins on the south side. Both had blank rear walls and uncurtained side and front windows; I took my time approaching each, the .38 held down tight against my right leg. The cabins' window glass was cleaner, and quick flicks of the flash beam showed me sparse furnishings, no indication of occupancy.

The direct route to the other two cabins was across open ground. I didn't care for the idea of that, so I went the long way—back through the trees, across the front of the garage, around on the far side of the store. Unnecessary precaution. The farthest of the north-side cabins was identical to the opposite pair, inside and out. The nearest cabin was dark and silent as well, but with a difference: the curtains were tightly drawn across both windows. I eased around to the door and tried the latch. Locked as tightly as the garage.

As I started back to the store, a car pulled in off the highway. I halted in the shadows as it rolled over to the gas pumps, but it was nothing for me to be concerned with—a battered DeSoto, the finned variety, driven by a lean young guy in a cowboy shirt and straw hat. His attention was on the pump when I came around the corner and went inside.

Adam Manganaris was back on his stool, eating a candy bar in little nibbling bites. He had loose false teeth, and on each bite they clicked like beads on a string. He didn't stop eating as I approached him, said through a mouth full of chocolate, "Didn't find anything, did you."

"You told me all the cabins were empty. Why are the curtains closed in one of them?"

"That's where I live."

"Is that right? Alone?"

"Wife died eight years ago."

"No relatives staying with you?"

"Don't have any relatives. All dead."

"You have a son."

"No one, here or Down Under."

"What part of Australia are you from?"

"Town near Brisbane. Why?"

"How long have you lived in this country?"

"Thirty-some years. Thirty-five, about."

"So Harold was born in Australia."

Instead of answering that, he took another bite of the candy bar. The sound his dentures made seemed subtly different to me now: the clicks were more like those of a revolver's hammer cocking, then falling.

The bell over the door tinkled, and the guy in the cowboy shirt entered. He went to a side-wall cooler, extracted a six-pack of beer, brought it to the counter. "Hey, Adam," he said. "How you been? Gettin' much?"

"Only what you're missin', mate."

Cowboy Shirt thought that was pretty funny. When he finished laughing he said, "Fifteen gallons unleaded. And a pack of Marlboros to go with this brew."

Manganaris served him, rang up the sale.

"Only what I'm missin'," Cowboy Shirt said, and laughed again, and went away and left us alone.

I said, "How much per night for one of your cabins?"

Surprise animated the cloudy eyes briefly. "Why?"

"I'm tired and I need a place to stay."

"Here?"

"Why not? Unless you have a reason not to rent me a cabin."

Manganaris thought about it. "Forty dollars," he said.

"Fair enough."

"In advance."

I laid two twenties on the counter. He made them disappear into the cash register before he produced a key on a chain attached to a four-inch block of oak. The numeral 4 was burnt into the wood.

"Number Four the one next to yours?"

"No. Second in line across the way."

"Nice and private."

"Right. Nice and private."

"There a cafe or truck stop nearby? I haven't had dinner yet."

"None open now. Closest is in Hollister."

"I don't feel much like driving that far. You have any packaged sandwiches?"

He gestured to the side-wall cooler. Skimpy selection: egg salad, lettuce and tomato, ham and cheese. I took the ham and cheese, added a small bag of potato chips from a rack on my way back to the counter.

"Nothing to drink?" Manganaris asked.

"Hot coffee, if you have it."

"No hot coffee."

I went and got a half-pint of milk. He rang up the sale, I paid him, he made change and bagged the items with his good left hand. Deliberately, then, he turned his back on me and picked up and opened one of the hardback books. I caught a glimpse of the title. *A Masque of Mercy* by Robert Frost. An Australian country storekeeper who read pastoral American poetry. Well, why not? People don't fit into easy little stereotypes. I knew that as well as, if not better than, anyone.

In the car, I called Kerry and told her where I was and that I was staying the night and didn't know yet how long I would be away. She'd spoken to Tamara so she knew how some of the day had gone; I filled her in quickly on the rest. I told her not to worry, and she told me to watch myself, and when I hung up I felt very much alone.

I drove down to cabin four, parked in front, and locked the car. Inside there was a bed, a dresser, a nightstand, a twenty-year-old TV on a stand, and a single sturdy-looking chair. I closed the curtains, bolted the door, set the chair under the knob for added security. The Colt Bodyguard I laid on the nightstand. Then I sat on the bed and ate my meager dinner: half the sandwich, a few of the chips, most of the milk.

It was quiet there, the highway far enough away so I couldn't hear the traffic sounds. I kept listening and hearing nothing but an occasional creak or rattle or wind whisper. After a while I lay down, the meal like a clot under my breastbone, and wondered if I were wasting my time. I didn't think so. There was something for me at the Outback Oasis—either Dingo himself or a line on his whereabouts. I was convinced of it.

And yet I could not quite get a handle on the old man. Why had he kept saying that he had no son? Knew what Dingo was and was ashamed of him? Maybe. But then why hadn't he been more straightforward with me? Why force me to play cat and mouse?

I got up and took a quick shower in mostly cold water and turned out the lights and slipped into bed in my underwear, transferring the .38 to a place under the second pillow where I could get at it more easily. And then I lay there, listening and waiting.

Nothing happened.

Eventually I slept, jerked awake at some sound, real or imaginary, slept and woke and slept and woke for most of the night. Toward morning, I slept soundly for a couple of hours. Nothing had happened, nothing was going to happen—and nothing did.

22

RESTLESSNESS DROVE ME OUT OF BED AND INTO my clothes at seven o'clock. With the gun in my coat pocket, I went outside for a look around. The morning was clear, chilly, and empty except for a couple of passing cars. But Adam Manganaris was up; his cabin, like the store, was outfitted with a woodstove because smoke drifted from a squat chimney.

I walked along the driveway, taking my time, and cut over along the side wall of the garage. The first of the windows was too dirty to see through even in daylight, but at the second I found a fairly clear spot on a lower pane. One of the vehicles inside was a dented, rusted pickup that no doubt belonged to the old man. The other, what I could make out of it, had the right lines to be an Olds Cutlass. I couldn't be sure, though, and I couldn't see the license plate.

I considered breaking in, but if Adam Manganaris caught me, it would give him a means to get rid of me and end the stalemate. Besides, it didn't really matter if the car was Dingo's Olds or some other make that belonged to him. There wouldn't be anything left in it to tell me where he was. The only way I was going to find that out was from the old man.

Brace him again now? No. Let him stew awhile longer, give him something to think about.

Back at cabin four, I left the key inside and then started the car and let it warm up, revving the engine in case he hadn't already been alerted. The door to his cabin stayed shut. After four or five minutes, I drove out to the highway and turned west toward Hollister.

It took me a while to find a cafe. Coffee, orange juice, some toast. Two refills on the coffee. And then a leisurely return trip to the Outback Oasis. The whole process took the better part of two hours. It was just nine o'clock when I parked near the store.

Manganaris had already opened for business; the Open sign was prominent in the window. Inside I found him on his stool, reading. Nothing changed in his expression when he looked up and saw me. He seemed just as listless and stoic today.

"So you're back," he said.

"You think I'd gone away for good?"

"Didn't think much about it at all."

Sure you didn't. "You're open early," I said.

"Nine to nine, every day except Monday."

"Long hours, unless you have an employee."

"Just me. At my age, what else am I going to do with my time except read and eat? And I can do those here as well as anywhere."

I said, "I took a look inside your garage this morning."

He didn't say anything.

"Through one of the windows. The car in there belongs to your son."

"Think so, do you?"

"Where is he, Mr. Manganaris?"

No response.

"I'm not going away, you know. Not today or any day until you tell me where he is."

No response.

"He murdered my client in cold blood, a woman who never did him or anyone else any harm. Forced her to lie facedown on her bed and pressed a gun to the back of her head and executed her. He did the same thing to Jay Cohalan. Would have done the same to me except that the gun jammed. That's why I won't go away."

Emotion, like a ghost image, flickered in his eyes and for an instant changed the shape of his expression. He said, "The bloody gun jammed on you?"

"That's right. By the grace of God. Otherwise I wouldn't be standing here right now. You believe in God?"

He nodded.

"How about justice?"

Another nod.

"Then tell me where Harold is. Put an end to this before it's too late and he kills somebody else."

"He won't kill anyone else," Manganaris said.

"He might. He's psychotic, whether you want to believe it or not."

"I believe it."

"Well then?"

For almost a minute he looked at me, or through me, without blinking. Then he said in blunted tones, "You win, mister. No point in lying to you anymore. It's the same as lying to myself."

"Where is he?"

"I'll take you to him."

"Just tell me where I can find him."

"No. I'll take you. My way or not at all."

I weighed it on both sides. If I pushed him, he might change his mind and close off again. And with the old man along, there would seem to be less chance of a violent confrontation. Unless this was some kind of trap. To look at him, frail and dispassionate, with that crippled wrist, you wouldn't take him for a dangerous or deceitful man. But Dingo was still his flesh and blood. Some men would do anything, anything at all, to protect a loved one.

I said, "You know that I'm armed."

"Figured you were."

"I won't hesitate to use my weapon if I have to."

"You won't have to."

"No?"

"He don't have his gun anymore."

"What happened to it?"

"I've got it. In my cabin."

"How'd you get it away from him?"

No reply.

"Is he hurt in some way? Sick?"

"You'll see when we get where we're going."

I would not pry anything more out of him there, that was plain. And I intended to make the trip no matter what the situation; this q. and a. was only prolonging things. I said, "All right," and Manganaris hoisted himself off the stool and came out from behind the counter.

While he reversed the sign in the window, I took a good look at his clothing: rumpled pair of slacks, white shirt, old, patched pullover sweater. The sweater was tight enough around his thin torso so that a concealed weapon was unlikely. He could have had a hideout gun strapped to his ankle under a pants leg, but that was paranoid thinking. In his arthritic condition, with that bad wrist, how could he hope to get at it and then use it?

Outside, I asked him as he locked up, "How far do we have to go?"

"Not far."

"I'll drive, you tell me where."

We got into my car. He directed me east on the highway, and we rode in silence for a few miles. Manganaris sat bent-backed, eyes straight ahead, hands gripping his knees. In the bright daylight, the knobbed bone on his wrist looked as big as a plum.

Abruptly he said, more to himself than to me, " 'Home is the place where.' "

"How's that again?"

" 'Home is the place where, when you have to go there, they have to take you in.' "

"Sounds like a quotation."

"'Tis. From a poem by Robert Frost, 'The Death of the Hired Man.' You read Frost?"

"Not since I was a kid."

"I like him. Makes sense to me, more than a lot of them."

Home is the place where, when you have to go there, they have to take you in. The words ran around inside my head like song lyrics. No, like a chant or an invocation—all subtle rhythm and gathering power. The nature and meaning of the quote were plain enough. Now I knew something more about Adam Manganaris, and something more about his relationship with his son.

We turned off on a county road, traveled another couple of silent miles through sun-struck farmland. Alfalfa and wine grapes, mostly. A private farm road came up on the right; Manganaris told me to turn there. It had once been a good road, unpaved but well graded, but that had been a long time ago. Now there were deep grooves in it and weeds and thistles and tall grass between the ruts. Not used much these days. It led along the shoulder of a bare hill, then up to the crest. From there I could see where it terminated.

The Outback Oasis was a dying place, with not much time left. The farm below was already dead—years dead. The buildings were grouped alongside a shallow creek where willows and cottonwoods grew, in the tuck where two hillocks came together: farmhouse, barn, two chicken coops, a shedlike outbuilding. Skeletons now, all of them, broken and half-hidden by high grass and shrubs and tangles of wild berry vines. Climbing primroses covered part of the house from foundation to roof, bright pink in the sunlight even at this time of year, like a gaudy fungus.

"Your property?" I asked him.

"My brother and me built it with our own hands," he said. "Frank came here from Down Under in the fifties, when the land was cheap hereabouts. Bought a parcel big enough for both of us. Took him ten years to convince me to join him. Raised chickens, alfalfa, apples, the both of us. You can see there's still part of my orchard left."

The apple trees numbered a dozen or so, stretching away behind the barn. Gnarled, bent, twisted, but still capable of producing fruit. Ignored and long-rotted fruit.

"Frank died twelve years ago," Manganaris said. "My wife, eight years ago. That was when I moved to the Outback. Couldn't stand to live here without Betty. Couldn't bring myself to sell the place, even so." He paused, drew a quavery breath, let it out in a kind of whistle. "Don't come out here much anymore. Twice a year to visit her grave and Frank's grave, is all."

There were no other cars in sight, but I could make out where one had angled off the roadway and mashed down an irregular swath of grass not long ago. I followed the same route when we reached the farmyard. The swath stopped ten yards from what was left of the farmhouse's front porch. So did I.

I had my window rolled down, but there was nothing to hear except birds and insects. The air was thick with the moist smells of growing things. I watched the house's front door; it stayed shut. And a tattered shade over the one facing window remained motionless.

"He inside the house?"

"Around back," Manganaris said.

"Where around back?"

"Beat-down path over yonder. Follow that."

"Not alone. You come with me."

"No need for that."

"Both of us, together."

He said, "As you'll have it, then," and eased himself out through the passenger door. I had the .38 drawn and down against my leg when he came around to where I stood. He saw it and said, "Told you, mate, you won't need that."

"Just lead the way."

He set off stiffly through the tangled vegetation. I followed at a wary distance, keening, trying to watch everywhere at once.

Nothing made noise, and nothing moved but the two of us. A faint fermented-apple smell came to me as we rounded the house to the rear; bees swarmed back there under the trees. Near where the orchard began, the path veered off toward a huge weeping willow that grew on the creek bank.

"Over there," the old man said. "Under the willow."

Graves, three of them.

Two were old and well-tended, marked by marble headstones etched with words that I didn't read. The other was new, the earth so freshly turned some of the clods on top were still moist. That one bore no marker of any kind.

I jerked my head around to stare at Manganaris.

"Now you know," he said without emotion or irony. "I didn't lie to you when I said I have no son."

I did not know what to think or feel. It was like being electrically shocked: confusion, temporary disorientation. I heard myself say, "He's dead? Why didn't you tell me he was dead?"

"Wanted you to see the grave for yourself."

"How do I know he's really in there? Some kind of trick. . . ."

"Dig him up if you're a mind to. But I won't help or watch if you do."

He wasn't lying; it was not a trick. The truth was plain in his face, in his voice—a darkling thing.

"How long has he been dead?"

"Three days."

Three days. All the running around I'd done, all the tension and anxiety and hungry anticipation and driving need, and the whole time Dingo, Harold Manganaris, the man who'd murdered me . . . dead and buried himself. No confrontation now. Nothing now, finished now. Dead, goddamn it, dead dead dead.

"How did he die?"

"I shot him," the old man said.

"*You* shot him?"

"With my old service pistol. Two rounds, one through the heart."

"Why, what happened?"

"He brought me trouble and heartache, same as before."

"Put it in plainer words."

A little silence. Then, "He was bad, Harold was. Mean and wicked from birth. You said it true this morning—psychotic. Stealing, breaking up property, taking drugs, hurting other boys. Hurting his mother." Manganaris held up his crooked left arm. "Hurting me."

"He did that to you?"

"When he was eighteen. Broke my arm in three places. Two operations, and the wrist still wouldn't heal proper."

"What made him do it?"

"Wanted money, I wouldn't give it to him. So he hurt me to get it. I told him before he ran off, don't ever come back, you're not welcome in my house again, you're no longer my son. And he didn't come back. Not until last Sunday."

Dead and gone. Dead under those clods of dirt beneath the willow. I still could not seem to come to terms with it.

"He wanted money again, is that it? Tried to hurt you again when you wouldn't give it to him?"

"Punched me in the belly," Manganaris said. "Still aches when I move sudden. So I went and got my pistol. He laughed when I pointed it at him and told him to get out. 'Won't shoot me, you old fuck,' he said. 'Your own son. But I'll sure as hell shoot you if you don't tell me where you got your money hid.' Then he showed me that gun of his. Two of us standing there pointing guns at each other, like in a bloody cowboy movie. Makes me sick to remember it."

Won't shoot me, you old fuck. Lay still, you old fuck.

I said, "What happened?"

"He tried to take the pistol away from me and I shot him. Once, in the chest. Stopped him, but only for a second. Then he shot me."

"Shot you? But. . . ."

"His gun jammed. Didn't go off."

". . . My God."

"That's right, mate. That's the real reason I brought you out here, why I'm talking to you like this. He killed both of us, Harold did, only God stepped in and we're both still alive. I reckoned God put the job of vengeance in my hands, so I fired again—shot my son through his evil heart. I didn't know then about the people he'd murdered. When I found out, I was all the more certain I'd been God's instrument, but after what you told me this morning. . . ."

He rubbed his face with gnarled fingers. Now I understood that look in his eyes, the one I hadn't been able to define. It was pain, and it was blood. Another bleeder, Adam Manganaris, the same kind as me.

"I loaded his body into my truck," he said, "drove out here, brought him to the creek in a wheelbarrow, dug the grave, and buried him. Hard work, hardest I've ever had to do."

"Why bury him next to his mother and your brother?"

"Told you before. 'Home is the place where.' I had to take him in, didn't I? For the last time?"

I walked away from him. Not going anywhere, just needing to move. How *did* I feel? Relieved, yes. And a little angry and let down, the way you do when you've been cheated out of something that was rightfully yours. For Adam Manganaris it had all ended with a bang; for me, with a whimper. No confrontation, no satisfaction in helping to put Dingo away in a cage, no sense of personal vindication. Yet it was stupid to feel that way. There were no guarantees that I would have been able to bring about the finish I'd envisioned; that more blood, my blood, would not have been spilled. The bottom line was that Harold Manganaris had paid for his sins without anyone else except this poor old man being harmed. Closure, Kerry had called it. Right. Justice served, case closed.

Manganaris was standing under the willow, looking down at one of the graves. When I rejoined him I saw that it was his wife's and that there were tears in his eyes. The moist earth and rotted-apple smells seemed to have grown stronger in my nostrils; the skeletal buildings and fungoid primroses were ugly reminders of death. I did not want to be here any longer—not another minute in this place.

"We'll go back to the car now," I said.

He nodded, wiped his eyes with the back of one hand. "Then where?"

"The car first."

We retraced the path, buckled in. I jammed the .38 into the dash clip and then backed the car around and drove fast up and over the hill without a glance in the rearview mirror. Neither of us spoke until I turned off the county road onto the highway.

Manganaris asked then, "You planning to notify the sheriff?" Matter-of-factly; not as if he cared.

"No," I said.

"Why not?"

"Your son's dead and buried. I don't see any reason not to leave him right where he is."

"But I killed him. Shot him down like a dog. I deserve punishment, eh?"

Old and dying like his crossroads store, like his farm. Precious little time left. Where was the sense—or the additional justice—in forcing him to leave the Outback and die in prison? But all I said was, "Not by anyone on this earth. God's instrument, you said. All right. We'll let God make the final judgment."

23

WHEN WE GOT BACK TO THE OUTBACK, Manganaris seemed reluctant to quit the car. He sat motionless, staring at his knobbed wrist. Without looking at me he said, "I've got a gift bottle of whiskey in my cabin."

"A drink at this hour? It's not even eleven."

"I know."

"And I don't use hard liquor."

"Neither do I," he said.

He opened the door, lifted himself out, moved away in slow, arthritic steps. After a few seconds, I shut off the ignition and followed him.

His cabin was cluttered with possessions, mostly books. While he hunted up the whiskey and a couple of glasses, I sat at an oval table and watched him. It struck me then, for the first time, that he was not very much older than me. All along I'd been thinking of him as an old man, but there could not have been more than a dozen years separation in our ages. If he was old, what did that make me?

The whiskey was single-malt Scotch in a dusty, unopened bottle. He broke the seal, poured two fingers for each of us, lowered himself into a chair across the table. He still wasn't looking at me, as if he'd grown too embarrassed to make eye contact. He didn't want to be alone, but he didn't really want me there, either. Neither of us had anything more to say.

Pretty soon I picked up my glass and drained it. The Scotch went down easily, trailing smoky heat. So easily that I craved another. But I wouldn't have one, not now and not ever again.

Manganaris hadn't touched his. He was staring away from me, at something not in this room—something long ago and far away. His eyes were full of blood.

I left him in silence and got into my car and went away from there. Once I was on the highway, moving at speed in the direction of Hollister, I began slowly to uncoil inside. And my thoughts grew as clear and sharp as they'd ever been.

Maybe the law would get onto Dingo and come around asking his father the same sort of questions I had. I hoped not, but if they did he wouldn't tell them anything; I was the only one he would ever share his secret with. Maybe Annette Byers would recover and provide details of the murders and make noises about the missing money; maybe Grant Johnson would be forced to tell about me after all. And maybe Fuentes would hound me for a while whether I decided to turn the seventy-five thousand over to him or not. But none of that seemed to matter much right now, one way or another. It was all little more than echoes of a period of sound and fury that signified nothing.

Four things had come out of that period, and as far as I was concerned only those four were meaningful.

I had survived.

I had finally stopped bleeding—unlike Adam Manganaris, who would continue to bleed until the day he died.

The clicks were fading, and with the passage of enough time, they would stop haunting my waking hours.

I could not, for any reason, go through something like this again.

When you boiled that last one down, it meant that Kerry had been right and I had been wrong. It was in fact the answer to my morning-after question of how, in what profound way, I'd been changed. My work was no longer the only thing that defined and sustained me; I would not shrivel up and die without it. I was sixty years old. I was tired mentally as well as physically. I was sick of pain and sorrow and blood; of dealing with lowlives like Dingo and Byers and Cohalan and Steve Niall and Charlie Bright and Nick Kinsella and Jackie Spoons and Zeke Mayjack and the drunk at the Blacklight Tavern. The time had come to pull back, look elsewhere for satisfaction and peace of mind. I'd had a good long run, done pretty decent work for more than thirty years. I could take pride in my accomplishments, and I had nothing left to prove, to myself or to anyone else.

I'd known all this for some time now at the center of myself, maybe even before Harold Manganaris put that gun to the back of my head, and I was finally able to admit it and to act on it. Tomorrow I would have a long talk with Tamara, start making arrangements for her to take over primary control of the agency and for the hiring of someone to do the fieldwork. The sooner there was an ending here, the sooner there would be a new beginning.

I thought about Kerry, Emily. How much I missed them, how much I needed them, how much I owed them. And I drove a little faster.

Home is the place where.